Mail-Order Teacher

Sarah Lamb

Contents

To all teachers, everywhere, thank you for your incredible sacrifices and dedication.

Chapter 1

Cottonwood Falls, Kansas, 1871

With a sniff and a quick glance around him, Samuel Donner alighted from the stagecoach, tugged straight his jacket hem, and tried—unsuccessfully—to brush the dust off of his sleeves. Dust flew around him in a near fog, stinging his eyes, soiling his clothes, tickling his nose, and covering his formerly shiny boots.

But that was nothing new. It had been that way for days. What *was* new was the unexpected fact that Cottonwood Falls, Kansas, a town far smaller than he was used to, was about to get an educator of his quality.

They were incredibly fortunate in this town, and Samuel hoped they realized the fact. A teacher of his caliber, with the extensive educational trainings that he had, was not common here in the West. No, he was no young woman, barely graduated herself and now teaching those she'd been in school with. He was educated far beyond anyone here, and intended to whip this school into shape, turning out well-equipped students as his contribution to bringing civilization to the West.

And judging by the looks of this sleepy little town, he was more than needed. Samuel pinched his lips together and shook his head. It appeared he'd arrived not a moment too soon. He could hear the distant sound of children laughing, yet from his vantage point, the schoolhouse was empty.

Who was in charge? Was it the end of the school day already?

He motioned the driver of the coach toward his bags and watched as they were set on the stagecoach platform. He had two with him. The rest would arrive later. The stage drove away in a cloud of dust, and the plume reached toward the heavens. His eyes burned once more.

This town had *entirely* too much dust.

An older man approached, one hand raised in greeting. "Help with your luggage, sir?"

"Yes," Samuel said, as he dabbed at his eyes with a now-stained handkerchief. "Can you have these delivered to the schoolmaster's cottage?"

"Ah." The man scratched behind his ear. "We don't got no cottage here for the schoolmaster."

Samuel straightened. If there was no cottage, the accommodations must be more fitting to a teacher's elevated station. Wonderful! That was fine news, and the first he'd had in a while. He could make allowances for this dusty little town. It was not like they could help Mother Nature's gifts.

He smiled at the man. "Is that so? Well, a house perhaps?" At the man's headshake, he asked, a touch of suspicion now filling him, "Then where does the head of the school reside?"

The man's face lit up then, in understanding. "Well, the board, there's three of them, they live in town. Usually, they host the teacher. Used to be the teacher lived with the families, moving every two weeks. That were a mite hard on all involved, so the board now provides the room and meals."

"Is...that so?" Samuel felt every bit of distaste on each syllable.

He turned and surveyed the town. Why had he come? The place didn't even have proper lodgings. Had he but known before the coach left, he might have gotten right back on it. Boarding with students? That wouldn't work out for anyone! But perhaps the school board members would remedy the situation. It was likely they'd never realized what was and wasn't proper in terms of housing for someone as educated as he.

"No matter," Samuel said, turning back to the man. "I'm sure things can be sorted quickly in a satisfactory outcome for all parties involved."

"I suspect so," the man said, scratching at his scraggly beard. Then, he waved his arm wildly as his face lit up. "Mrs. Miller! Mrs. Miller! Over here!"

Samuel watched as a woman turned, then approached. He didn't bother to hide the curiosity on his face. Who was she?

"The new teacher is here," the man before him said. "Didn't know we were having one. Seems a mite confused where to go. Uses a lot of them big and fancy words."

"New teacher?" The woman looked just as puzzled as Samuel felt. "But, I didn't send away for one yet. I'd intended to, but hadn't posted the letter. There must be a mistake."

Was this what he was to expect from the town? Such difficulty with the adults' comprehension made it obvious why they had difficulty with student retention and education.

Frowning, Samuel reached into his coat pocket and produced a letter. "I have here something that says otherwise," he told her. "In fact, are you Isadora Miller?"

"I am!" She smiled at him then, giving him a long look he wasn't quite sure was entirely appropriate. He'd have stared back, perhaps jar her and show it was rude, but he had the distinct feeling that wouldn't make a bit of difference to this woman.

Mrs. Miller was tall and thin, almost painfully so. Her oversized hat seemed ridiculous in this environment, and was covered in so many feathers it appeared as though an entire flock of birds was upon her head. Graying hair peeked beneath, but it was her eyes, the sharp, piercing, almost predatory gaze she fixed upon him that he disliked. He decided the hat suited her.

"I have a letter from you, madam," Samuel said. He offered the envelope.

The man, who had not given his name yet, leaned forward to squint. "Why, that's your handwriting, all right," he agreed, nodding at the woman.

"Hush, Willy," the woman said, and plucked the letter from Samuel's hands. When she opened and read it, she brought a hand to her face. "My goodness. I can't believe it."

Samuel waited, his lips pressed together. He regretted being here already. If it hadn't been for the fact the letter had struck a chord within him, made him feel the urgent need to come, he'd have looked for another place. He wished now that he had. These people in their small town didn't quite seem to know their left hand from their right. What would the students be like?

"Why, this *is* my letter," she said, her head bobbing and her hat wobbling, "but oh dear. I must have gotten my letters mixed up. We'd not sent away for a teacher just yet. If you got this one...then, where did I put the one asking for a mail-order husband?"

Husband? Samuel's head jerked up.

"What a thing to have happened. Well, we do need a teacher," Mrs. Miller mused as she tapped the letter in her palm. "This letter is truthful in the fact. But I'd hoped to introduce my niece Abigail to a husband." She apprised him carefully. "You'd have done nicely. But, unfortunately," she continued, "I'm afraid I can't do that and kill two birds with one stone, because she might have someone interested in her now."

Thank goodness. The less I have to do with this strange woman and any of her family members, who are undoubtedly like her, the better.

"However, isn't it fortunate things have worked out as well as they have?" She smiled at him, and took his arm. "Willy, send those bags to my place. The new teacher will be staying with me."

As Samuel opened his mouth to protest, to ask for proper accommodations, perhaps at a boarding house, she quickly added, "I've a room for you, and it's all quite appropriate. I've hosted several teachers," she said.

"Several? Why have you gone through several?" he asked, feeling himself being pulled along.

"Who knows?" Mrs. Miller answered as she guided him down the street. "Providence, perhaps, as it's brought you here."

"I shall endeavor to do my best for the school board and the students," Samuel answered, concern taking root at the possibility these children might be more than a handful if they'd run off several teachers. "You mentioned truancy in the letter. I don't abide by that."

"Oh! I do love a man with a firm resolve," the older woman said, and gave a girlish giggle. "You are just so cute."

They stopped before a small white house, her, Samuel, and Willy. Willy set Samuel's luggage down and left.

"You will make a fine teacher for our school," Mrs. Miller said, and patted his arm before reaching into her reticle to unlock her door.

But before he could answer, she added, "And since Abigail has someone interested in her now, I think you'll make me a wonderful husband!"

Chapter 2

Closing her eyes, Abigail Lees let her shuddering sob release, then righted her shoulders, pulled at another weed in the vegetable garden, and tried to lose herself in the never-ending chores.

Jim had been gone a year now. When she'd become his wife, it wasn't supposed to be like that. They'd only been married for two years. She was Jim's second wife. He'd had three children from his first, but she'd died in childbirth, bringing forth their last child.

Abigail's marriage to him had been one of convenience. He was in desperate need of someone to care for his children. She was in desperate need of leaving her aunt's house. So, when he'd proposed his idea, she'd said yes without thinking.

Of course, it would have been impossible not to love the children. They adored her, and she was grateful. She hoped she'd been a good ma to them. Thomas was now eleven, Sally was seven, and Little Jim was five. They were good children, helping her as much as they could, but the simple fact of the matter was, Abigail was ill-equipped to provide for three children on her own, both financially and physically.

Jim had gotten the fever and ague. By some miracle, it had passed by the rest of them, but it had happened so quickly, there was scarcely time for her to register his illness. However, the last almost year had been near unbearable, as Abigail discovered that Jim had only just provided for the family, and there was nothing set by.

The house was owned, at least. However, chances were she'd need to sell it to take care of the children. But if she did, what would she do once the money ran out? And where would they live?

Abigail glanced up at the sun. The children would be home soon from school and could take over the weeding while she continued some of the other things that needed to be done. Her back ached, so she looked forward to that, but weeding was good. It helped the garden, and allowed her to pull out the weeds with all of her fury.

Almost every week for the last two months, Old Mr. Sampson had stopped by, telling her how they should marry.

And when Abigail said old, she meant it. Mr. Sampson was at least three decades older than her. She had no desire to marry him. She wasn't that desperate.

Yet.

But what if she got to that point? What if that was the only way to provide for the children? She prayed it wouldn't come to that. So far, they'd managed. By some miracle, the small box of coins they had in the kitchen never ran out, even if it was low. She had no idea how that was, but was grateful for it.

The sound of laughter and running feet made Abigail look up. The children were back. She bit her lip in consternation as she noticed their bare feet and clothes that were getting ragged. She had to get them new clothing and shoes. But how?

Another problem for another day, she told herself, and stood, greeting them with arms wide for a hug. "How was school, my darlings?" she asked.

"We have a new teacher, Mama," Sally told her. "He is very strict."

"Then you must be on your best behavior, and try your hardest," Abigail said.

The children chattered away about this and that while taking over the weeding. Once they'd told her about their day, she left them and headed to the house to check on dinner. As she stirred the pot of beans and made sure the bread was cooking evenly, Thomas brought a pail of milk inside.

"Thank you," she told him.

"I'm man of the house." He shrugged. "It's my job."

"I appreciate it," Abigail said, "though you are still my boy, and I wish you didn't have to work so hard."

"I don't mind," Thomas said, and went back outside for his next chore.

Abigail watched him go with a heavy heart. She never imagined being twenty-six, widowed with three children who biologically were not her own, and alone in the world. Her aunt, though she lived nearby, wasn't of any help. She was flighty, and the last that Abigail heard, seeking a man for her own financial stability. Perhaps she saw Abigail as an obstacle to that, and that's why she never offered assistance.

The next few hours flew by. Dinner was finished, homework started, and Abigail was just starting to yawn. The sun wouldn't set for at least another hour, perhaps two, but she was still tired. One woman, doing the work for two, was exhausting.

As she listened to Little Jim say his letters, the lull his sweet voice was creating was broken by a sharp rap at the door.

"Now who could that be?" Abigail wondered. She moved to the door to open it, and took in the man before her.

"Mr. Donner?" Sally asked in surprise. "Mama, this is our new teacher."

Abigail looked at the man. He was dressed quite unlike anyone she'd ever seen, and it was apparent he wasn't originally from this area. His shirt was a pristine white, he wore a burnt orange colored jacket, and his pants were a cream color and also clean. Brown boots, shined to perfection, nearly gleamed. He seemed the type of man who cared very much about appearances.

"Good evening," Abigail greeted politely.

"Madam," Mr. Donner said. He glanced past her. "I came to discuss your children. And to introduce myself to you, of course."

"Oh?" Abigail raised her eyebrows. This Mr. Donner was quite unlike the last teacher had been. Or the ones before her. He seemed stiff, aloof, and she hoped he genuinely wasn't that way, or else he'd find his lovely clothes splattered in muck by some of the rowdier children.

"Yes," he answered.

"Please, come in," she invited, and motioned to a chair at the table. "You already know my children. Thomas, Sally, and Little Jim."

"Actually," he said, sweeping past their faces as his head turned quickly, "I do not have the pleasure of having met Thomas. In fact, according to the records left by the former teacher, Thomas hasn't been attending school."

"What?" Abigail looked from him to Thomas. "There must be some mistake."

"Truancy, madam, is a mistake that will cost greatly. Children must be educated. I have come here to find out if you are withholding a proper education from your son."

Abigail stood there sputtering. Finally, she collected herself enough to say, "Absolutely not! How dare you accuse me of such a thing." She stood and pointed to the door. "Teacher or not, sir, I won't have you come into my home and accuse me of such a terrible thing. We will have this conversation at a later time. When you are wearing your manners, along with your fancy clothes."

Mr. Donner gaped at her for a moment, as if he couldn't believe his ears, but Abigail put one hand on the door and pointed again. He walked out, tugging down the sleeves on his jacket. "We will have this conversation once *you* have calmed down," he told her as he strode past.

Abigail didn't answer. She slammed the door shut, then spun around to face her children. Each of them was staring at her, mouth wide open. "Finish your homework," she ordered, and then let herself outside, going through the back door.

The cool evening air helped to lessen her hot temper. She hadn't meant to be a poor example for her children, or leave a bad first impression on the teacher. But his accusation! It was false, she was sure of it. Thomas was a bright boy. They had many difficulties within their home, but school attendance was not one of them.

Abigail glanced up as the sun started its descent. Oranges and reds bleeding into pinks filled the sky. It was beautiful, but there was no one to share it with. There was also no one to share her hurt over the new teacher's words.

Mr. Sampson's visit today came back into her mind. She didn't like the man, but she realized that he was correct. Perhaps the teacher's visit had proved it. It was obvious she was overworked and overwhelmed. Abigail was a single woman. How much longer would she be able to take care of herself and her children or their small farm without help?

Chapter 3

Samuel stood in the doorway of the one-room schoolhouse, quickly surveying to make sure all was as it should be before the students arrived. It was a surprisingly nice school for such an area. Eight large windows let the light into the room, and the large pot-bellied stove sat in the middle, unlit for it was summer, but already filled with wood.

His desk was neat, and behind it on the wall was the portrait of George Washington, and—crooked. Samuel strode across the room, adjusted the frame slightly, and squinted. Yes. That was better.

He returned to the doorway and picked up the brass bell about the size of his hand. He rang it sharply six times, and took his position at his desk.

As each child came in, he marked their name down in his attendance book. After opening with the pledge of allegiance, they began lessons. Copying out letters for the younger ones, copying spelling words for the oldest, on their slates.

Samuel walked around the room, hands behind his back as he looked down at each child. He spent an extra moment next to Thomas Lees. The boy's copywork was excellent. His lips pursed, and he continued his circuit of the classroom.

As he taught history, and later math, to the fourteen pupils under his care, he kept looking at the boy. He was glad he'd attended school. Perhaps the visit to his mother had scared them both into proper behavior. Now, he just had to do that for the other eleven students missing.

Recess was a noisy affair, as was to be expected. The girls played with jump ropes, the boys with balls. Samuel watched from his desk as he allowed himself the luxury of letting his thoughts wander.

The caliber of the school's interior surprised him, but in a pleasant way. When he first toured the school, he was worried he might find a dirt floor, only high benches and no desks, and perhaps no teaching tools at all. That said, from what little he'd seen, though extraordinarily dusty, Cottonwood Falls seemed a respectable and thriving town. They even had a doctor of some caliber, he was assured, Doctor Edward Mason, with a wife who was also medically inclined.

It was a good thing, as he might one day need their assistance. Yesterday evening, after he'd returned from the Lees home, he'd nearly been attacked by Mrs. Miller. He'd hurried through his dinner, using the excuse of having to prepare his lessons, but she'd taken every opportunity to flirt with him—something he found quite unsettling.

More than once, as he'd been in his room, a chair before the door just in case the woman got some strange idea to burst in, he'd regretted coming. But each and every time he'd thought about leaving, like the long line of teachers before him, he knew he couldn't.

It was about more than a job. More than simply bringing order to the tardiness in the school. Samuel firmly believed—and knew firsthand—the value of a good education. He was determined any child under his tutelage would receive one. Where the others before him had failed, he would not. He'd promised himself and the school board, and he wouldn't go back on his word.

Samuel let his eyes roam across the schoolyard, ensuring all was well. They stopped on Thomas Lees. The boy was sitting, shoulders slumped, head downward. Oh, he had no doubt the boy would rather be playing hooky, perhaps wading in the stream and collecting tadpoles. But as teacher, it was Samuel's job to see to his educational needs. There was plenty of free time to be found at that age.

Perhaps that was the issue with the other missing children as well? They didn't have caring parents? To be sure, it was a fact here in the West that the labor of children was needed, especially in farming families. It was true, without help during harvest or planting, a family might starve. However, right now was neither.

Determination welled inside of Samuel. He'd make sure to impress the importance of education on each family. Starting with that Thomas boy's mother. How dare she! Had he not been so shocked at her poor behavior—which was obviously where the boy got it from—he'd have argued his point.

He let his gaze return to the book in front of him. There wasn't much to do once school ended other than visit parents, but he hoped he could find more once that task was complete. Truth be told, he was not looking forward to returning to Mrs. Miller's home afterward. However, he'd not been teaching long enough to expect the town to offer him different accommodations. He'd also not gotten his pay yet, to look into boarding houses.

There was one thing Samuel was sure of, and that was he flat out refused to marry Mrs. Miller. The idea was preposterous! By her own admission, she'd later confessed she hadn't been interested in him. Just because he was there, and she'd mixed up something or other and mistaken him for a mail-order husband didn't mean that's what he was.

Her new desire for a husband was not something he intended to remedy. She could send away for another husband. Surely, one would be willing to take her, but it wouldn't be him. Besides the fact, he had no interest in marriage.

Samuel checked the time and then rose. His long legs carried him to the schoolroom door, where he rang the bell six times, then strode back to his desk, mindful to count each child as they returned.

"Open your readers," he told them as he moved to the front of the classroom.

The final two hours of school went quickly, and he dismissed the class, then gathered his list of student homes he wished to visit.

As he walked down the schoolhouse steps, Samuel wondered if he should go back to the Lees house. Just as quickly, he decided against it. He had no desire to be scolded again.

"Mr. Donner?"

The soft voice caught him off guard, and Samuel looked up, then blinked in surprise to see it was the woman he'd just been thinking about. "Madam," he greeted stiffly.

"I want to apologize to you," Mrs. Lees said. "I was rude to you yesterday because...well, it doesn't really matter.

I shouldn't have been and nothing excuses my poor manners."

"I...appreciate that," Samuel said, cautiously.

"You see." Mrs. Lees stopped, took a deep breath, and said, "I'm sorry. I have no excuse, even if my mind wants to make one to explain what life has been like as of late. Please, accept my apology and join us for dinner tonight? It won't be fancy, stew and bread, but it's some way I can properly make things up to you, but also listen to what you had to say."

She continued, "I did not know about Thomas. Thinking over it today, I now have my suspicions where he has been during school hours, but I hope I'm wrong. He is a good boy. So are his siblings. They've had things very difficult, and while that's not an excuse for his behavior, but perhaps a sign I need to try harder, I won't know what's going on until I find out."

"I would be happy with a supper of stew and bread," Samuel answered, accepting her olive branch. "To speak candidly, I suspect I will have far more meals with Mrs. Miller than I'd enjoy."

"Mrs. Miller?" Mrs. Lees's mouth formed a small circle, and he was startled to realize at how perfectly shaped her lips were. And how he'd noticed.

"Why, that's my aunt," she said in surprise.

"So, you are Abigail?" he asked.

"Yes. How...do you know that?"

He pressed his lips together, debating telling of the secret horror he'd shouldered on his own. He finally decided to confess it. After all, this was a small town. He'd rather the story come from his mouth than Mrs. Miller's.

"It appears your aunt sent away for a mail-order husband," he started.

"She did?" Mrs. Lees stared at him in shock.

"At the same time," he continued, "she also planned to send for a teacher. Somehow, her letters got mixed up, she claims, and I received the request to become teacher, but she's under the impression I'm to be her husband. I don't understand how that happened. Truthfully, the entire scenario makes no sense to me, but that is how she presented it."

"But why would my aunt want to have a mail-order husband?" Mrs. Lees asked. She shook her head. "I always assumed she and Willy, over at the stagecoach office, would court. He's had his eye on her for years."

"I wasn't to be her husband," Samuel said. Then, before the words could find their way to his brain to stop the utterance of them, he continued. "I was to be yours."

Chapter 4

Abigail didn't know what to say when the teacher revealed how her aunt had sent away for a husband for her...and it was meant to be him. Should she laugh? Run? Stare at him in complete...well, she wasn't sure what she felt. Only that she couldn't believe, after all that had happened, sending away for a mail-order husband was her aunt's plan.

As a matter of fact, the two had hardly exchanged words over the last few years. They might as well be strangers. The two of them had never gotten along well, so the fact her aunt had even considered helping her find another husband was a surprise. Was it because she didn't want Abigail to land on her doorstep with three children?

No matter. She wouldn't be getting married to anyone. Not if she could help it. Especially someone who walked around calling women "madam" and looked down their nose at others! Where did Mr. Donner think he was from? No, it sounded like she'd escaped something just as unwelcome as Mr. Sampson's proposal.

But...how long could she hold out? The children might not be hers by blood, but they were by love, and were her responsibility. Foisting them off on someone else or an orphanage had never, ever crossed her mind. Providing for them, though, that was a constant worry.

She sighed and looked out the window at the children playing outside. Thomas was letting Sally chase him and catch him in a game of tag. Little Jim was laughing and cheering her on.

Abigail glanced at the table. Five places were set. It had been a while. To be sure, it felt awkward to have the teacher over for dinner, but she did need to apologize. Show they had manners. Even if it was possible the teacher did not.

She glanced around the kitchen once more, then ran through the front entry and the sitting room to be sure she'd picked up everything and it looked neat. The teacher already had a bad impression of her; she didn't need to increase it.

Outside, the children's shrieks and laughter had stopped. A moment later, Sally burst in. "Mr. Donner is here," she announced.

Abigail smoothed her hands down her front, then yanked off the stained apron, balled it up, and put it on the kitchen counter. She hurried to the front of the house.

The teacher stood there, looking slightly uncomfortable. Regret filled Abigail. She'd caused that, and that she'd been thinking slightly uncharitable thoughts about him. "Welcome, Mr. Donner," she said. "Please, come in."

"Madam," he said, and walked inside.

It was all she could do not to smirk or roll her eyes at the word.

"Dinner is ready," she said. "Children, go wash."

The three hurried over to the bucket in the corner of the kitchen and made short work of their task. Abigail motioned to the table and a chair, "Please, sit," she told their guest.

He nodded and sat, and the children hurried over as well. Sally sat next to him. Abigail brought over bowls of stew and set them down. "Help yourself to the bread and butter," she told the teacher.

"Thank you," he said.

They ate in silence for a moment, before Mr. Donner said, "It was good to see Thomas in school today."

"My son goes every day," Abigail said, feeling a little offended that once again the teacher was commenting on this. "His father was strict on that. I also understand that education is important."

"It is," the teacher agreed. His tone was wary. "But according to the records of the previous three teachers, Thomas's attendance has been scarce."

She shook her head. "I don't know how that could be." Hesitating, because if there were a total of four teachers saying the same thing, perhaps it was true, she looked at Thomas, then at Sally and Little Jim. "You all leave for school together. You do...all attend, don't you?"

There was some guilt swarming her at her question, but since Jim had passed away, life had been such a never-ending blur of things to do, she sometimes struggled to do the necessary things, and the children had been taking themselves to school.

When there was no answer, Abigail fixed the three with a look. "I asked a question," she said quietly, sensing something was being hidden she wouldn't like. "I want the truth."

It was Little Jim who answered. "We go, me and Sally. Thomas don't always."

"Doesn't," Abigail corrected. "He doesn't always go. And why not, Thomas?"

"I don't want to tell you," Thomas said, looking down at his stew. He shoveled in a bite, and kept his head low.

"Is it you dislike your lessons?" Abigail asked. "Do you have trouble with them?" She drew her brows together. He had always loved learning. Had something changed? A difficulty he was ashamed to admit?

"No, ma'am," he answered, still not meeting her eyes.

"Today, Thomas showed he was an astute student," Mr. Donner complimented. "Everything he did showed he's a clever boy. Though he is behind, I have every confidence he will catch up quickly, and exceed my expectations."

Abigail noticed the teacher's eyes flicking between her and Thomas. She disliked having this conversation with someone who was a near stranger, but it felt important. After all, he was the town's teacher. "What is it then?" she asked quietly.

Thomas swallowed hard, then looked up at her. "I do jobs. So I can make money. So that you can feed us and not send us away to an orphanage."

"An...orphanage?" Abigail gasped. "What on earth would give you such an idea?"

"When Pa died, our last teacher said that's what you might do, because then it would be easier for you to find a husband." Thomas's eyes filled with tears.

"Then, that old man who comes around. The one who wants to marry you. He don't want you having kids. He just wants you because you're pretty. Could be he sends us away to an orphanage, and then we'll be without a ma twice."

His words were choked out, and his face turned a shade of red, indicating he was trying to hold back either anger or tears. Abigail wasn't sure which.

Abigail got up from her seat so quickly it scraped along the wood floor. She wrapped her arms around the boy. It was obvious to her that he was hurting deeply. "I'd never do that," she told him, and then looked at Sally and Little

Jim. "You three are quite stuck with me. I'd never give you up. I told your father I'd care for you, and I do. Not because of the promise I made him, but because I truly love each of you. As for the job..."

Abigail shook her head. If she told him they didn't need the money, he'd know it was a lie. So, she took a deep breath and said, "The care and providing for is my responsibility. Going to school and helping me at home is yours. You must promise me you'll attend classes, Thomas."

"Yes, ma'am," he answered, head low.

"I'm sorry," the teacher said quietly.

Everyone looked at him, as though they'd forgotten he was there. She had, actually. There was a look of regret on his face. It was almost curious of her to see it. Gone was any trace of pretentiousness. There was only compassion. Embarrassment.

"It's my job, what I was hired for," he explained, "to get students back into the classroom. There's a significant truancy problem. Truth be told, I only thought about the fact that, this time of year without harvest or planting, students might just be skipping school for more enjoyable pursuits. It never occurred to me they might have a meaningful purpose."

He looked at Thomas. "What you are doing is noble, young man. But your mother is right. Attending school is your job."

Then, he looked at Abigail, concern in his eyes. "I know that I am new in town, but if your financial position is anything I can help with—"

"No, no," Abigail said quickly, hoping that the absolute mortification she was feeling right now didn't show. "We are fine. Will be fine. Thank you, though."

Abigail rose from where she had stooped, gave Thomas a squeeze on his shoulder, and turned her back to the table for a moment. "Let me get the dessert," she said lightly, "while you children tell me what else you learned today."

Sally cheerfully told a story about another little girl during recess, and Abigail took the moment to slice the apple pie, collect her thoughts, and then whip the cream for the pie's topping.

Now she knew why there was always just enough. The coins came from Thomas, sacrificing his education and childhood in a desperate attempt to keep his family together. She just wished he hadn't mentioned Mr. Sampson. Would he really get rid of the children if she gave in, for their sake, and married him? That was the only reason she'd do it.

Abigail was heavy in her thoughts as she set the pie in the center of the table, and asked Mr. Donner to serve it. As she turned to get the whipped cream, she found it hard to breathe. What was she to do?

She sat back at the table and forced a smile on her face. Sally was still chattering away, and her story had Little Jim and Thomas in laughter. It lightened her heart a little, but when she glanced up, Mr. Donner was looking at her with such a look of sympathy, it nearly undid her.

The marriage was her backup plan. But now...there was even more risk than she'd originally thought. How would she provide? What could she do?

Abigail shivered, and drew her shawl about her shoulders, but she knew it wasn't a chill in the air, it was fear that had wrapped itself around her in a terrible squeezing vice, and she wasn't sure if it would let her go.

Chapter 5

"Very good. You may sit down." Samuel watched the student return to his desk after successfully reading the primer in his hand. He glanced down and put a checkmark next to the child's name. So far, his visiting the parents of the truant students had returned all but four students to the schoolhouse. One was ill, another sorely needed to care for an injured parent, and the other two had moved away.

He felt pleased with his increase to the schoolroom. The school board had also approved. Single-handedly, Samuel had done just what was needed—restored the students and brought order to the classroom.

There was one person, however, who he knew didn't have his approval. Thomas Lees. The boy had taken every opportunity to scowl at him that day.

"Students, you may go and have your lunch and recess," Samuel announced. "Thomas, would you stay just a moment? This won't take long, and then you may join them."

The other students noisily grabbed their lunch pails and baskets and hurried out into the sunshine. Thomas sat, a worried look on his face. "Am I in trouble?"

"Not exactly," Samuel said, and squeezed into one of the small desks nearby. His knees pressed against the desk's top. "I wondered if you might explain something better to me," he asked.

"Last night, you'd talked about a man wanting to marry your mother. But you also said something about losing a ma twice. Being new to town, I'm afraid I don't know everyone's history, and I am feeling confused. I feel as though I'm missing part of the story that I ought to know, especially if there is some way that I can be of assistance. I am your teacher, but I also want to know you better."

"It was the truth," Thomas said. Then he burst out, "And if she has to marry that horrible man, it's all your fault!"

Samuel drew in a sharp breath. It was on the tip of his tongue to reprimand the boy, but instead, he practiced patience. Something all good teachers were required to have. And he was more than a good teacher. Samuel Donner was *exceptional*.

"Will you please explain that rationale to me?" he asked.

"Mr. Sampson is wanting to marry Ma. He's been coming by the house all the time since Pa died. He doesn't like us kids. I don't even know if he likes Ma. She sure doesn't like him. But I know she's worried about not being able to take care of us."

"I'm sure your mother will do all she can to prevent a marriage if she doesn't want one," Samuel answered. "Perhaps some extended family can help."

"We don't got no family," Thomas answered. Then he added, "That's why I've got to help. My family needs me."

"You don't?" Samuel asked, choosing to ignore the poor grammar. He also tried to ignore the pang of sympathy at the rest of the boy's words, though that was just as difficult. "What about Abigail's aunt? Mrs. Miller?"

"She's not my aunt," the boy said. "Ma isn't really our ma. I thought you knew that from when you had dinner with us. She married Pa when our first ma, our real one, died."

His voice lowered and trembled as he added, "She could leave us at any time. But I don't want her to. I mean, I guess I'm a man now. I'd be okay. I'm eleven. But Sally and Little Jim still need her."

Samuel closed his eyes for a moment, trying to take in all Thomas had told him. What a difficult situation for Abigail. And what an incredible woman she was, suffering and struggling to help three children not even hers. She deserved help, and kindness. Not worry.

There was no doubt in his mind, as he replayed Thomas's words, that the boy did need Abigail as his mother. He loved her. Eleven was far from manhood, though he'd never tell Thomas that. He'd done far more than a child should at his age. But he'd done it all for the sake of keeping his family together.

A strange lump formed in Samuel's chest, right near his heart. He looked over at Thomas. "If I can find a way to help you, I will," he said. "Let me think on this for a little. But if you have any ideas, please tell me right away. I want to do whatever I can."

Thomas wiped the backs of his hands across his eyes, and Samuel felt sympathy at the wet smear of a tear. "Don't wait too long," the boy pleaded, as he stared into Samuel's face. "That man's bad. I just know it."

"I promise," Samuel said. With some difficulty, he squeezed out of the desk and stood. "You go on out and enjoy yourself."

"Yes, sir," Thomas said, and was gone, lunch in hand, before Samuel had returned to his desk.

Taking out his own lunch, Samuel ate it slowly, debating as to the recent events. What was it he could do to help the family? His salary was not so large he could do much. Certainly not support an entire family, not yet. He was on half salary until he'd been there six months, and then it would be brought to full. He blamed all of the teachers who left too quickly for that. He should have been given far more than he was. Yet another omission from Mrs. Miller's letter.

Still, he could do something. He was sure of that, and he would figure it out. The increasing desire to take a room at a boarding house flitted through his mind again as he mentally went over his financial state.

Samuel had savings—a good deal, actually. He just didn't want to decrease them more than necessary. But it might be something he had to do soon. Living with Mrs. Miller was unbearable.

He'd suggested perhaps he move to one of the male school board member's homes, and she'd been very vocal that wasn't going to happen.

As school ended with his releasing the children for the day, he lingered as long as he could, then returned to Mrs. Miller's home.

She greeted him exuberantly. A new hat was perched on her head. One so filled with ribbon it almost looked like an elaborate cake. Did this mean she was leaving? He hoped so.

"Welcome, Mr. Donner," she giggled.

"Thank you, Mrs. Miller. It was a good day at the school," he said politely.

"Wonderful. We feel very strongly about education in our town, and I do love an educated man, such as yourself."

"Thank you," he answered, then winced that he'd replied to her compliment about him. "I do my best."

"I was just thinking again about how fine of a husband you'd make someone," she continued, not at all shy. She stepped closer, and her overabundance of perfume made his eyes water and his nose stuffy. "Namely myself. Do you prefer a spring wedding or summer?"

"Madam," Samuel said, holding his ground though he really desired to take a few steps back and open a window to clear the stench, "I did not come to Cottonwood Falls to marry."

"You might be surprised at what happens." She giggled again. "But I must leave you, I'm afraid. I've a ladies' meeting this afternoon and evening. I've got a cold supper laid out for you."

"I appreciate it," Samuel said with a small bow. He stopped when he saw her reaction of delight, and decided that was not something he'd do again.

Mrs. Miller giggled once more and turned to leave. He watched her go, letting out a loud breath once the door shut behind her. Samuel returned to his room, and settled himself with a small stack of papers. He'd given each of the older children one that morning and asked them to write about themselves, so he could get to know them better.

Of course, he planned to think about Abigail's problem, but first he needed to clear his mind. Perhaps focusing on work would do that. Interactions with Mrs. Miller jarred him in a most uncomfortable way.

Thomas was smart, he reflected as he picked up his gradebook. And the boy had a good heart. He truly wanted to help his family. So did Samuel, but he wasn't sure how—yet. Something would come to mind, though. It always did. While this particular situation wasn't one he'd ever faced, Samuel found it surprising that in a town such as this, one where everyone seemed friendly and kind to one another, that a woman such as Abigail would be left to fend for herself.

But...would she have? If the letters had been sent correctly, and, of course, only if he'd accepted, things might have been very different. He might have married Abigail, been there to help her with her situation. What would that have been like? He didn't know her well enough to speculate on it, but one thing he knew for certain was that she was a woman with a backbone. He liked that.

As he recalled his earlier conversation with Thomas, he felt a pang of sympathy and also kinship with the woman. In some small way, for he had no one dependent upon him, he understood how she felt. She wasn't the only one being coerced into an unwanted marriage. What would happen to him with Mrs. Miller's blatant pursuit? And what might happen with Abigail?

Chapter 6

Abigail shook the wet shirt and hung it on the line. There was a mild breeze, which would help it to dry faster. She'd spent the last two hours washing their clothing and bedding. After all of that scrubbing and bending, it was a welcome feeling to stand straight and stretch as she hung each piece.

There was no school today, and she'd allowed the children to chase minnows in the stream nearby. The water was low, so she wasn't worried about one of them getting hurt. They'd also more than earned the right, helping with the chores. Sally had taken a small pail with her, just in case they stumbled upon blackberries, as they sometimes did.

People passed in the distance, and Abigail glanced toward them. While she lived in the town, her home was set a short distance away. Close enough to see the comings and goings if she desired, but far enough to have some animals, a small barn, and elbow room that wasn't too close to anyone else.

She looked in surprise, though, as one figure off in the distance seemed to head in her direction. They were too far away to see properly, but she did know that it wasn't Mr. Sampson. He walked with an almost rolling gait. This individual strode with purpose.

Abigail continued to hang the laundry. Perhaps she was mistaken, and the person would pass by.

But, they didn't. Two sheets, three dresses, and one shirt later, the person was clear enough for her to see it was the new teacher, Mr. Donner.

Her heart sank. What did he want? Had something happened again? Feeling nervous, she smoothed the front of her dress and pushed back the strands of hair she knew had escaped, then wondered why she'd done that.

"Madam," the teacher greeted as he entered the yard.

"Abigail," she said. "Abigail is just fine."

Mr. Donner looked at her for a moment, hesitated, and said, "Very well. Samuel, then."

"Samuel," she said, enjoying the feel of his name on her tongue. It rolled off nicely. "I hope all is well?" she asked, hesitatingly.

"It is," he assured her, and she felt herself relax slightly. "I'd like to make you an offer. Perhaps two, if you'll allow me."

"Oh! Of what kind?" she asked. The wind gusted just then, and a sheet threatened to tangle around her. She stepped away, and motioned to the house's porch. "Would you like to sit?"

"Thank you," he said.

They walked to the porch, where several benches and a rocking chair sat. The teacher settled himself, then leaned forward, his eyes intent. For some reason Abigail couldn't explain, her heart sped up. She felt nervous, but stopped herself from fidgeting.

It was a good thing he wasn't there to marry her. She likely would have felt all tongue-tied. The teacher's mind was sharp. Quick. His eyes piercing as though they knew a great deal. She admired that intelligence. Could admire it too much.

"I'd like to offer to tutor Thomas in the afternoons or evenings," he started. "To make sure he knows all that he needs to know and gets caught up. He's a very clever boy, but he has missed a good deal of school."

"You...you would do that?" Abigail asked, sure there was surprise in her voice.

"Of course. I'm his teacher." Samuel shrugged, and flashed a grin that made Abigail grateful she was sitting, or else her knees might have wobbled. She realized just how handsome the teacher was, now that he'd seemed to relax a little.

"That would be kind of you," she said. "Thank you. We go over his lessons in the evening, and I admit, I'd be grateful to have one less thing to do." She studied him a moment. "You said two things?"

"Yes." He sat up straighter, and then hesitated, as if unsure how she'd answer. "I'd like to hire Thomas."

"Hire him? To do what?" she asked. Abigail was sure her eyes narrowed.

"The crates I had sent here from back east should arrive next week," he told her. "Inside are a good number of books and other educational items. It would be a great help to me to have him unpack, help make sure everything is there, and then store the items in the classroom, in the places they should be."

Abigail nodded slowly. "I see. Well, if Thomas agrees, I approve."

"I think if he could help me, perhaps an hour or two a day, it shouldn't take more than a week. Afterward, I understand a few of the local businesses are looking for someone to run errands a few hours a day. Perhaps he'd like to ask around."

Samuel stopped speaking, and looked at her with a concerned look on his face. "I know it's none of my business," he started.

Abigail tensed. Never once in her life had anyone ever said those words and then not proceeded to give their opinions on something that wasn't their business whatsoever. What would he say? Was it that she wasn't providing well enough? That she was a terrible mother?

"I understand someone has been pressuring you for marriage." He stopped, and seemed undecided as to if he should continue.

That wasn't what she'd expected, and Abigail startled. "It's true," she admitted, before she realized she'd spoken.

His eyes met hers, and filled her with a strange sensation. His face was open, earnest, even appearing as though he were struggling to compose himself—a complete contrast to the man she'd supposed him to be based on their past conversations. He seemed the kind of man she could—wanted to—tell her problems to.

"As much as a newcomer can, I would do all I could to chase them away," he added, "if it would help you in some way."

Abigail shook her head, a lump forming in her throat. When was the last time anyone at all had offered to help her? She really didn't know. Since she'd moved here, she'd always felt a bit like an outsider. A smile, a wave, but never a friendship with anyone.

She took a deep breath. "I appreciate it. Yes, it's true. I...don't welcome the idea of marriage from that man. I am grateful for your offer, but please, don't trouble yourself. Things will work out, I'm sure." She glanced away in the direction she knew the children were, then back at him. "I confess, I'm near the end of my rope, and considering accepting the offer or perhaps simply taking out my own ad for a husband, though I don't want to."

He nodded. "Is it because of the children?"

"Yes." She spoke softly. "I promised their father to always care for them. But," she waved an arm around, "it's too much for one person. It's all I can do to put food on the table. I've even thought of selling the house, but then we'd be in the same position again soon, only without a home." She took a shuddering breath. "It's not ideal, but I am a woman alone and without options."

"Is...there no one else?" he asked. Then, the teacher's face burned crimson. "Forgive me," he said hastily. "That was inappropriate."

Abigail laughed. Bitterly, but still a laugh. "No, I'm afraid not. No one wants a woman with children already."

"That's foolish," he said, and startled her into meeting his eyes again. "There is something noble about protecting those who need it. A woman with children isn't less in any way whatsoever. Perhaps she is more. She has knowledge and wisdom and patience within her from the challenge."

Her lips twisted, almost in amusement. His words were so seriously spoken. She'd never heard someone so surprised, almost indignant on another's behalf. "Nobility is something there isn't much of out here. Dust, drought, poor crops, an abundance of families joining our fair town...that we have aplenty. Even in this lovely town, the men are few. I've even thought perhaps of being a mail-order bride. But what if I took the children into an unsafe place?"

"That wouldn't be good," he agreed.

"Not just that," Abigail said softly. She didn't know why she wanted to admit the truth, but it tore from her as though it were forcing itself past her lips in a rush to stop her from stifling it. "I'd like love. If that's possible. I know that sounds foolish, but..."

"Love," he repeated, and this time it was Samuel's turn to gaze into the distance, a considering expression on his face. She watched him, obviously deep in thought, and marveled at the tiny flickers of emotions dancing on his face. Was love something he had ever had?

A moment later, he looked back at her. "That's important," he agreed. "I hope you find it." He stood then, and asked, "Might I come tomorrow for a lesson?"

She nodded wordlessly, standing and watching him as he left. Abigail stood there, near frozen to the spot until the teacher turned into a speck that eventually vanished behind a building.

She shook herself, then hurried back to the laundry. The wind picked up again, fluttering the dresses on the line. It was the same feeling she had in her stomach as Samuel had looked at her. Really looked at her. What did that mean?

Chapter 7

Samuel could feel Abigail's eyes on him as he walked away. He wanted to turn, but also didn't want to see whatever expression might be on her face. He wasn't sure where they stood just now. It was obvious she had some mistrust. Perhaps thought him a foe and...someone who brought chaos to an already difficult situation?

But his situation wasn't feeling much better. He dreaded his return to Mrs. Miller's home. The offer of tutoring Thomas was, in truth, a good idea for the boy. But it also bought him time away from the woman. Something he couldn't get enough of.

Which reminded him that he didn't want to live in her house a moment longer than he needed to.

Samuel paused at the boarding house that one of the children had pointed out to him. It wasn't very large, but according to the boy—because he had no intention of asking Mrs. Miller—it was the only place in town. He walked up three small steps onto a small porch, knocked, and left a short time later, lips pressed together and a headache forming. There were no vacancies. Worse, there was a waiting list for a room! At least he was on it now. There was some small hope.

Had all of the other teachers had to board with Mrs. Miller? If so, perhaps that's why they'd left so quickly. He couldn't imagine she was easy to get along with.

He started toward the general store, intending to get a few things. When he pushed in the door, the shopkeeper was busy, talking to another man. Since he was in no hurry, Samuel took his time, going over to a shelf of books. Perhaps there was one he'd not read but would enjoy.

However, as he browsed, he realized everything on the shelf was either something he'd already read, or had no desire to. Such as some sort of romance story. Romance. That wasn't something he had any interest in. He came to Cottonwood Falls for one reason only—to teach the children. Not find love. Though, it seemed someone was intent on pursuing him to bring their own romance story to life.

Samuel shuddered. Did Abigail react the same way about the man who she said was interested in her? He thought so. She'd mentioned she had no interest in him. Did that mean there was someone she was interested in?

Or was she simply too busy to even find the time to consider such a thing?

He couldn't help but feel slightly worried for her. It was obvious she was struggling, but refused to give up. He admired that, but knew full well how desperation could oftentimes lead to choices that one didn't welcome. Would she get to that point? He hoped not.

She was an attractive woman and—and when had he started to think about that? Abigail was the mother of three children he was the teacher of. Nothing more. His concern over his students' education was spilling over into the domestic situation, and he needed to put a stop to that. Her life was her own. His was his. He had a job to do, and that's just what he would be doing.

He blamed her aunt for the whole situation. Yet...he found himself enjoying Cottonwood Falls, and, if he were to be truthful, the less tense conversations with Abigail. What might it be like to just spend an afternoon with her? Bring a smile to her face?

Foolish thoughts.

Samuel moved over to a collection of bound books with blank paper. Yes, now one of these he could use. He looked carefully at the sizes and colors of their covers, choosing which would meet his needs best. Snippets of conversation between the store owner and the customer reached his ears.

"...good land. A good location too. There's some of the best proximity to water, fertile ground, all right near town. You know how much they'd pay me if I sold it?"

"That's not your land, though," the shopkeeper said mildly.

"Not yet," the customer agreed. "But once I marry her it will be. Abigail Lees won't keep saying no. I'll press her until she can't do nothing but marry me."

"I don't know," the shopkeeper said. Samuel shot a glance his way and saw the man shake his head. "Doesn't seem right. She's been through enough. Besides, I don't think she wants to marry you."

"Sure she does," the man argued. "Just playing hard to get. Women like to do that. Never you mind. Maybe I'll keep the place. Not certain yet. But I'm pretty sure with my plan, I can have both the land and a pretty wife."

"What's your idea?" the shop owner asked. "We don't need trouble in this town."

"Then I better not tell you what it is," the man laughed, and turned to leave. He nearly walked right into Samuel, but continued past without a word.

"Hello, Mr. Donner," the shopkeeper said as the shop door closed. "Help you with something?"

"I'll take these two books," Samuel said, placing them on the counter. "A few pencils too."

Then, he glanced at the closed door. "Who was that?"

"Oh, old Mr. Sampson. You heard? All talk, that one. Mrs. Lees won't marry him. Don't know why he's insistent she will."

"Sounds like he has a plan to make her," Samuel said, hoping his tone was one of nonchalance. He pointed to a jar of peppermints. "Handful of those too, please."

"Nah, as I said, all talk." The shopkeeper wrapped the peppermints in a cone of paper and twisted the top closed. "Anything else for you, Mr. Donner?"

"No thank you," Samuel answered.

"That'll be two dollars and eleven cents."

Samuel set the money on the counter, took his items, and left. Though the shopkeeper hadn't seemed worried, Samuel was. He wasn't sure Mr. Sampson had been all talk. There had been something in his face when he turned around that showed the man was serious about what he had said. He wanted the land, and Abigail.

His earlier thought came to mind. Desperation leading to choices. Just how desperate was Mr. Sampson for the land, and Abigail as his wife?

Being new to town, Samuel didn't know the man too well, but he couldn't help but wonder. How far would the man go to get what he wanted? And was Abigail able to protect both herself and the children?

He hadn't wanted to insert himself into the middle of her life, but something told him that he'd greatly regret it if he didn't.

Chapter 8

As always, there was more to do than time and energy. Abigail was exhausted. That was nothing new to her, though. Since Jim had died, that feeling was one that had stayed with her. A small voice inside of her head told her that it was likely that wouldn't change if she married Mr. Sampson. He seemed the type to expect to be waited on. He would want her to do everything.

She carried a basket of potatoes into the barn, loaded them into a sack, and returned to the garden. Thomas was making furrows in the soil Sally and Little Jim had helped dig a short time ago. They'd be planting mid-season seeds, and hopefully have a little more to harvest.

The fear of being unable to provide food for them this fall was a genuine worry for her. She'd been so concerned, she'd tried twice to visit her aunt, but the woman was never home. The idea of becoming a mail-order bride was getting more appealing. There were many good men in the world. Perhaps her letter, her plea for shelter and kindness, would land with one.

Abigail was so lost in her thoughts, she didn't notice when Mr. Donner—Samuel—walked up to the garden fence. "Hello," he greeted her.

"Oh!" Abigail said. She'd forgotten the teacher was going to come and tutor Thomas. She wiped a stray hair from her face, then groaned internally when she saw her dirty hands. It was likely her face was now smudged.

"Gardening, hmm?" the teacher said, as he released the small latch on the gate and let himself in.

To Abigail's surprise, he moved next to Thomas and squatted beside him. "What are you doing?"

"Dropping seeds in the holes," Thomas said.

"How many do you do in each?" Samuel asked.

Abigail watched quietly. It was an odd question, and she wondered why he asked it.

"I do two in each," Thomas said.

"I see. How many holes are there?" Samuel questioned. "How do you know how many seeds you need from the store?"

"Ah." Thomas frowned. "I don't know. I just usually count as I go along, and hope I have enough?"

"Let me show you a math trick," Samuel said. "It works just as well as counting one at a time, but it's faster."

Abigail quietly let herself out of the garden, not wanting to interrupt their lesson. About an hour later, she was surprised to look through the house window and see Thomas and his teacher carrying baskets of carrots and onions to the barn. How had they gotten so much harvested?

She went outside and offered them a bucket of ginger water. It was something Jim had taught her to make, so that a person who had been working hard didn't get sick feeling from drinking so much water to quench their thirst. Jim had told her it was also called haymaker's punch. She preferred the name ginger water, and thought it sounded nicer.

The recipe was quite easy. It was water, of course, dried ginger, apple cider vinegar, and something to sweeten it. Today, she had used molasses.

"Thank you, Ma," Thomas said, drinking deeply.

Samuel also drank, and offered his own appreciation. Abigail was surprised to note that his usually impeccable appearance was anything but. His forehead was damp, his shirt was wrinkled, and his pants had dirt on the knees, but he smiled at her in a way that made her cheeks flush, though she didn't know why.

"Thank you for all of your help in the garden," she said, redirecting her thoughts. "I wasn't expecting that, but I am incredibly grateful to you."

"Nature provides many opportunities for education," Samuel said. "In fact, if Thomas enjoys fishing, perhaps when I come next time, we can try our hand at that? It would be good for him to learn the food chain of aquatic creatures, but also about their skeletal systems."

Thomas wrinkled his nose. "I'm not sure if that sounds like fun or like work," he admitted. "But I'd like to try. Maybe we can even catch a bunch and salt 'em for the winter."

"Maybe we can," Samuel agreed, as he put a hand on the boy's shoulder.

"Would you like to stay for supper?" Abigail asked. "We've plenty."

"Say you will!" Sally cried out as she rushed over. "Hello, Teacher."

"Hello, Sally. I'd be delighted to accept your invitation," Samuel said. "But I must wash first." He looked up at Abigail. "Is there anything else you need help with?"

The question caught her by surprise, and she shook her head. "No, thank you. Children, please show Mr. Donner where to wash, then you can all come into the house once you are clean."

She watched as the children surrounded him and led him the short distance away to the washing pail and soap. With a smile she wasn't sure why she wore, Abigail headed back inside and set the table.

A few minutes later, she set a crusty loaf in the center of the table, and then a potato and corn stew. Orange carrot chunks colored the dish, and everyone ate heartily.

As conversation started, Sally asked, "Mr. Donner, you are so good in the garden. Maybe you should be a farmer. Why did you become a teacher?"

He laughed, and the warm smile he flashed Sally made Abigail's stomach do a little flip. "There's a story behind that," he told them. "But I'm not sure it's very interesting."

"A story we've never heard is always interesting," Little Jim said, looking at him. Abigail didn't miss the expression of adoration on his face. It appeared her children liked the teacher. Now that he'd gotten accustomed to the town, was he perhaps more relaxed, and the kind of teacher the children thought was fun?

"Well," he began, setting his spoon down, "it all started when I was a boy."

"You were once a boy?" Sally asked skeptically.

"Yes, I was. Can you believe it?" Samuel shook his head and flashed a grin at her. Then, his expression became sober. "When I was growing up, I didn't have parents who cared if I went to school or not, so, for a very long time I didn't go. I figured, why should I waste my time learning numbers and letters and things like that, when I could be out exploring and having fun?"

"That's a good question," Thomas mumbled around a bite of bread.

"I had an older brother who also didn't go to school much," Samuel continued. "While I didn't go to school often, I knew how to read. I knew my basic numbers. He didn't know anything. In fact, he made fun of me for how I liked to learn. Well, one day, we were standing outside of the schoolhouse. We'd do that sometimes, trying to convince one of our friends to join us at the stream instead of staying at his desk.

"The teacher started telling a story about a far-off place. I was fascinated. I'd never heard such a thing before. My brother was bored and tried to pull me away, but I wanted to stay and listen."

"And did you?" Sally asked.

"I did. What I didn't realize was, is that the teacher knew I was there. Well, he left off at a sudden point in the story, and promised to finish it the next day. So, do you know where I was?" Samuel asked.

"You went back and listened!" Little Jim guessed.

"I did. I stood outside the window and heard the rest of that story and part of another. It happened like that every day for a week. Until on that Friday, the teacher leaned out the window and asked why didn't I come inside and learn even more things the following Monday." Samuel smiled. "And that's just what I did. Once I got into that schoolroom, I didn't want to leave. It was like a new world had opened before me. One I just couldn't get enough of."

"What happened to your brother who didn't want to learn?" Thomas asked.

Samuel's expression grew thoughtful, and his words were slow as he answered, "While I was fortunate I had a desire to learn and improve my mind, a child who does not, or does not see the value in education will perhaps turn to bad ways."

"Is that what happened?" Thomas asked.

"Yes," Samuel said heavily. "One day, he stole something from a store. It hadn't been the first time, the shop owner claimed. By this point he was older, near adulthood, and his punishment more severe."

"Where is he now?" Abigail asked.

Samuel drew in a shuddering breath and closed his eyes as a pained expression washed over his face. He opened them again a moment later. "He's not with us anymore," he said quietly. "His justice was doled out in a permanent way. And it's often I wonder if I should have tried harder. That's why I'm so strict," he continued. "I might have failed my brother, but I won't fail my students."

His words filled Abigail with a heaviness, but she understood now why he was the way that he was. As the children started being silly and giggling over a story Thomas was telling them, she found herself looking deeply into Samuel's eyes.

She wanted to tell him he hadn't failed anyone, but the words wouldn't leave her lips. Instead, all she could do was stare, and wonder why she was dreading the moment he'd leave.

Chapter 9

Samuel shifted in bed, staring up at the ceiling. Somewhere, there must have been a leak because he could hear a soft plinking inside of the room, adding to the symphony of the rain outside. Usually, the sound of rain helped him to fall asleep. Tonight, however, his thoughts kept circling around to Abigail.

Did her roof leak? If it did, how would she repair it? Would she really consider a mail-order marriage? Just how desperate was she getting? He was terrified to ask, yet longing to know.

And as soon as he'd pondered each of those questions, his mind's eye took him back to the general store, where Mr. Sampson had seemed determined that both Abigail's land and Abigail herself would be his. The thought disturbed him. He wasn't sure if it was because he disliked the idea of that man potentially taking advantage of her or if it was because he didn't like the image of Mr. Sampson close to Abigail. Married to her, even.

Nearly three weeks had passed since the day he'd started to tutor Thomas. More often than not, Samuel stayed there for dinner. As time had gone on, it became comfortable. Relaxed. He almost felt as though he belonged there. While Abigail would bring things to the table, he'd start to dish them out or slice the bread, helping her.

It wasn't so much that he was trying to lighten her load, but that it felt natural. As though he belonged there in that role. Once, Little Jim had knocked over his cup, and he'd impressed even himself at his reflex to swoop it up and sop up the milk before it had fully registered to his mind the incident had happened.

After dinner, he started to read a story to the children. Abigail would sit there mending something or perhaps mixing bread dough and listen as well, a smile on her face.

It all felt so comfortable. So homey. Unlike anything he'd ever had before. Samuel began to crave going over there in the afternoons, and regret leaving as the sun started to set. It was something he'd have never thought would happen.

It seemed to him that Abigail also looked forward to seeing him, and had a little disappointment on her face when he had to leave.

Samuel was mindful to make sure there was nothing suspect about his daily visits. That it was obvious he was tutoring Thomas. But if small jobs got done to help Abigail, was that so bad?

It was still a surprise to him that he'd so freely told what little he had about his past, his brother. Usually, an overwhelming rush of pain filled him and prevented him from even going beyond a thought. For some reason he couldn't explain, the story had been pulled out. Would it, in any way at all, help Thomas to understand he wasn't cruel or a taskmaster when it came to educational needs? He wasn't sure. After all, Thomas wasn't avoiding school to play. He was doing it to put food on the table.

Samuel hoped desperately that the boy's love of learning would stay, and that he and his siblings would get to a place where they felt more assured in their safety.

The sun rose slowly, and the rain stopped. Samuel watched all of it through his window, not having slept one bit. As he swung his legs out of the bed, he stepped into a small puddle. So, that's where the leak was.

He dressed and hurried down the stairs. Mrs. Miller was already awake, and dressed in a mauve colored monstrosity with more ruffles and bows than not. The frills were so thick he marveled at how she'd fit through the doorway.

"Good morning, Samuel," she said.

"Madam," he replied, sitting at the small kitchen table.

"I've a lovely breakfast for you," she told him, beaming as she set a plate before him.

It *was* a lovely breakfast. Ham, eggs, oatmeal with molasses, and fried potatoes and onions. Samuel almost felt guilty at it. Many of his students arrived with very little for their noon meal. How many had a breakfast even a portion of this size?

"I've been thinking," Mrs. Miller said, sitting across from him. Her eyes were sharp, and he didn't like the look in them.

"Oh?" he asked, trying to remain neutral. Meanwhile, he was hoping against hope that several people would leave the boarding house so that he could have a room.

"Yes. I've decided that you are such a good teacher, there's no need at all for you to stop."

"Stop?" Samuel asked, a little surprise in his voice and the fork half raised. He hadn't realized she had wanted him to.

"Yes, I mean once we are married. You know, conflict of interest and all," Mrs. Miller said, waving around one of her hands. "With me being on the school board, I don't want you to think that you have to give up the very thing you enjoy, just so it looks proper."

Samuel set his fork down and opened his mouth. Before he could speak, she continued.

"You've no need to worry. I will arrange for everything," she assured him, then giggled.

"Madam," Samuel said, trying to keep his tone one of calm, and not display the internal panic that he felt, "I am not getting married. I have told you that."

"And I think differently," Mrs. Miller said smugly.

This was going to go nowhere. He tried to change the subject. "Mrs. Miller—"

"Isadora," she interrupted, and leaned forward, beaming at him. "There's no need to be formal."

"Madam," he said, "might I ask you a question?"

"Of course," she said.

"Abigail Lees is your niece, isn't she?" At her nod, he continued, "Then why do you not help her? It is obvious she is struggling."

Mrs. Miller's expression grew serious. A long moment passed, then another. Samuel wasn't sure she would even answer. Finally, she said, "I was going to. That's why I wrote the letter for the mail-order husband. You see…"

Again, she was so quiet, he wondered if she would speak.

"Abigail used to live here with me. She lived here for about two years before she married Jim Lees. It was a good marriage. She wanted a family, he had one. Of course, he had to go and die." Her lips pressed together.

Samuel was studying her as he ate, not speaking as he didn't want to stop the story.

"I'm not sure, really. I guess…I could do more. But Abigail has always been headstrong. Wanted to do things her way. I suppose that I decided to let her do just that. Manage things the way she wants to. Then we'd have nothing to argue over. We argued a good deal while she was here."

"I'm not sure she can manage much longer," Samuel said, shaking his head.

"We all have challenges in life," Mrs. Miller said briskly. She shrugged. "She'll find a way or else make one." She looked at him then, and her voice wobbled. "I know you've been tutoring her oldest boy, but don't you forget. You are mine. I've decided that. Though there was a mishap with the letters I'd written, the point remains. I sent away for someone, you are here, and I won't share. It is my turn for marriage."

Was that what this was about? She refused to help Abigail because she wanted her turn at a husband? Additionally, that she felt, in some way, jealous of her and the time that Samuel spent there? Samuel hardly knew what to say in his shock, other than the one thing that he had been repeating.

It was time, however, to make it clear, allowing no room for confusion, his role in Cottonwood Falls.

He stood from the table. "Thank you for breakfast," he said. A smile formed on her face and she parted her lips, but he spoke again and watched the smile droop.

"I am aware there was some misunderstanding about why I was intended to be here. However, I will fill one role only. As I have stated multiple times, I have no intention of getting married. Teaching is my job. If not here, then elsewhere."

He strode to the door, opened it, and looked back at her. "I'll await your decision, Madam, as to if I am to leave."

As the door closed behind him and he strode to the schoolhouse, Samuel felt irritation over every inch of him. This wasn't how he wanted to spend his morning after a sleepless night.

In truth, he also didn't want to leave. Didn't want to leave Abigail, that was. When he said he had no intention of getting married, it was to Isadora Miller he was thinking of. Abigail Lees, though...that was a little different.

Though they had started off on the wrong foot, something had happened, little by little, and they'd formed a sort of understanding, and it felt nice. Comfortable, though he knew he kept overusing that word. There was just no other way to put it. He felt, when he was with Abigail and the children, that he was home.

Samuel wasn't in any rush to lose that feeling, though he knew perhaps it was foolish. He didn't know how Abigail felt. For all he knew, she could still be considering the mail-order ads.

With a sigh, his long legs carried him to the schoolyard. He'd only gotten a few steps closer when there was a loud shout and angry voices. Turning his head, Samuel froze as he caught sight of young Thomas, being held by the collar and shaken.

Chapter 10

Abigail put the jar of butter she'd churned yesterday into her basket and covered it with a clean cloth. The baker gave her credit for any butter or eggs she brought. She hoped to be able to trade today for something as a surprise for the children and Samuel. He'd been a tremendous help around the house. Even though he was meant to be tutoring Thomas, that had turned into doing small jobs for her around the house and garden.

By this point, she was sure she'd be caught up on all that needed to be done by the fall, and also that her children would be some of the smartest around.

Samuel had started to teach each of the children above their grade levels. Sally was very clever with her numbers while Little Jim seemed to have a memory that held anything. He could recite facts and figures and places and names. Last night at dinner, he told Samuel how he wanted to be a teacher too. It had nearly rendered Samuel speechless, and he had swallowed a good number of times before telling Little Jim it was a fine profession to consider. Abigail smiled to herself at the memory.

Thomas was enjoying his studies too, and had developed a fondness for history. That was what he seemed to enjoy the most, though he did everything well. Well-rounded was what Samuel called him.

She drew closer to the town and then paused. The children had left for school about twenty minutes before, but there seemed to be a crowd clustered near the general store. Angry shouts met her ears, and Abigail hurried closer. If there was a problem happening in the town, she wanted to get to her children.

Her children. They were that, every inch as much as they'd been Jim's. More, now that she was the only parent they had.

"I didn't do it," a familiar voice shouted. "Please, Mr. Donner! Believe me!"

Abigail gasped, and then hurried forward, pushing her way through the crowd. Voices continued as she neared.

"Let the boy go," Samuel's voice, firm and authoritative, rang out over the buzzing of the crowd. "I'll take him into my care."

"Don't make right what's wrong," the shopkeeper said angrily. "My window is broken, and he was nearby."

"That doesn't mean he was the culprit," Samuel said calmly. "Who has sent for the sheriff?"

"He's away, visiting his folks," Mr. Sampson said as he stepped forward. Abigail could see his smirk, though she was still a short distance away. "We'll have to wait for him to settle this."

"And that is what we will do," Samuel said.

"Wouldn't have happened if that boy had a father." Mr. Sampson shrugged. Then, he turned and addressed the crowd. "I've been trying, but that woman is resistant. What kind of a mother is she?"

Abigail reached the edge of the crowd and gasped as she found herself the victim of every eye upon her. She tried to speak, but all that came out was a sputtering sound, blessedly covered up by the crowd's whispers.

"Thomas, go into the schoolroom and wait. Mr. Links," Samuel said to the storekeeper, taking control of the situation. "Why don't you explain what's happened? Mrs. Lees is here. This ought to be a discussion for us, not for the entire town. Let's go somewhere quiet."

"I don't see what you've got to do with it," Mr. Links said. "You aren't the boy's father."

Abigail was ready to answer when Samuel said, "I am not, but I am his teacher, a character witness, and in part in charge of his punishment when on school property, which he is right now, and where he was when he was grabbed."

The shopkeeper nodded. "Reckon that makes sense."

"Let's go see what the boy did," Mr. Sampson agreed.

"Might you show me and Mr. Donner first?" Abigail asked Mr. Links. "As he said, this is a matter for us. Not anyone else." She didn't miss Mr. Sampson's scowl, but after hearing what he'd said about her a moment ago, Abigail couldn't care any less. She was furious at the man.

The shopkeeper nodded, and walked to the back of his store. A window gave view of a small hallway by a staircase that led to the upstairs of the shop.

"See? It's broken," Mr. Links said. "Your boy was nearby."

"But did you see him break it?" Abigail asked. She twisted her hands. "Thomas has never been one to be destructive."

"I didn't," the shopkeeper admitted, "but he was here."

"That's called circumstance," Samuel said. "I'm not sure without evidence that much can be done."

"Is...is anything else damaged?" Abigail asked, forcing the words from her lips.

Mr. Links opened the door beyond and hesitated. "I...don't think so. But," then he stopped. "I had a medal from the war, my father's, sitting in a small frame on the wall." He pointed. "That meant everything to me. And it's gone now."

"There was nothing in Thomas's hands when I saw you with him," Samuel said. He stepped closer to Abigail. Though he didn't touch her in any way, his presence comforted her. Confusion and overwhelm filled her. She was fearful, both for Thomas and for herself, that she might say something she shouldn't. Anger was rising up in her. Thomas would never do such a thing like he was being accused of. Abigail was sure of that.

"I want to see Thomas," Abigail said quietly. As she and Samuel turned to the schoolyard, a small crowd was in front of the building. "Children," Samuel said, "You may have a half hour of nature search in the yard. I want you to form groups of two. Search for the colors of the rainbow. Collect your items if you can and be prepared to identify each species of the item you find."

Samuel pushed open the school's door and walked in, Mr. Links right behind him. Abigail rushed over to Thomas, who was sitting at a desk, his cheeks red, eyes swollen, and his face splotchy. He had been crying, and she pulled free her handkerchief to blot at his face before she wrapped her arms around him.

"I didn't do it, Ma," he told her. "I didn't."

"Can you tell us what happened?" Samuel asked gently. Abigail was relieved that he seemed to believe her son. Especially after she'd staunchly come to his defense before about him being in school, and it had turned out he had not been.

"We were walking here," Thomas said. "I kept feeling a prickling on my neck. Like someone was watching us. We were passing by the store, and someone came from behind us, I didn't see who. They went behind the store. I didn't think much of it."

He then looked apologetically at her. "I was trying to hurry us past. Mr. Links had put toys in the front window, and I didn't want Sally or Little Jim to feel bad we can't have them. Well, then we heard a crash. I told the kids," Thomas jerked his thumb toward the outside, "to get to the school and look for you, Mr. Donner. Just in case. Then I went around to the back and looked. The window was already broken."

"Thomas," Abigail said softly, "something was missing. It was taken." She paused, not wanting to say what she knew she needed to, but Mr. Links was glaring at him, arms crossed in front of his chest. "Did you take anything?"

"No, Ma! I didn't even touch the window. Was there something in it?" he asked.

"A liar," Mr. Links spat. "I'm sure of it."

Abigail drew herself up to her full height. "How dare you!" she said. "Thomas is not a liar. He's a good boy, and I'm ashamed that you don't realize that. What have we ever done otherwise to show our family was anything but trustworthy?"

Samuel calmly interjected, "We will get to the bottom of this. Your medal will be found, Mr. Links. Until then, let's send word to the sheriff. Thomas, you'll stay right with your mother or me, so no one can accuse you of anything else. Until we figure out what's happened, and until the sheriff returns, we will just stay calm."

"No staying calm about this," Mr. Links growled. "Boy's a thief. That's all there is to it."

He stalked across the schoolroom and slammed the door behind him. The portrait of George Washington shook, and became slightly off center.

Abigail turned to face Samuel, and was surprised to see him right there behind her. "What will we do?" she whispered.

"First things first," Samuel said. He knelt down and met Thomas's eyes. "I don't think it was you," he told her son. "And I'm going to do all I can to prove it."

Thomas nodded.

"Go ahead and join the others outside," Samuel said. "I'll start class in just a minute."

As soon as he went outside, leaving the school door open, Abigail turned to face Samuel. There was so much going around in her mind, she wasn't sure what she wanted to say. What she could say.

Samuel seemed to sense that. He put a hand on her arm, and gently said, "I believe him, Abigail. I'm going to help. Somehow."

Tears came from the rush of gratitude filling her. Abigail breathed in shakily. "Thank you," she whispered.

He didn't pull his hand away. Instead, he slowly moved down her arm and to her hand, where he held it in his.

She realized she was shivering. His warmth was the only thing that seemed to ground her. Without realizing it, she stepped closer. He squeezed her fingers gently, and Abigail couldn't pull her eyes away from his. They were gray. How had she never noticed that?

The air was heavy between them. Abigail felt as though she could hardly breathe. Samuel lowered his head and whispered, "I want to tell you something. I know," he swallowed hard, "it might not be the right time, but, Abigail, I think I am—"

"Mr. Donner?" a girl asked from the doorway. "Is class starting now?"

In an instant, his expression turned to that of Mr. Donner, the teacher, and no longer the Samuel whom Abigail had wanted to lose herself in

"Yes, you may ring the bell," he told the girl. "Six times, as I do."

As Abigail stepped away, the look he gave her nearly seared her in two. She moved toward the door, as he went to the portrait of George Washington, where he straightened it.

Abigail stepped outside and waited as Thomas safely entered the school. She watched for a moment through the open doorway. Samuel began to distribute books to the class. As he came to the back row, he glanced up, saw her, and smiled.

And she wondered, as she left the schoolyard to return home, just what he had been trying to tell her before they'd been interrupted. For a moment, she let herself wonder what if.

What if she could have his comfort each time she needed it? What if he was feeling something for her, the same way she was feeling for him. What if Samuel *had* been her mail-order husband?

Chapter 11

Samuel couldn't help but feel that Abigail was unfairly set upon by the people of the town that morning. He'd seen their judgmental looks toward her. Heard their comments. That Mr. Sampson hadn't helped. He seemed to take pleasure in strutting around and telling everyone how he'd been trying to help, but she was stubborn, and her children were too.

"Tame her then!" one man had called out.

Mr. Sampson had laughed and slapped his knee. Samuel had wanted to slap something else on him. Anger and disgust filled every inch of his body. How was it Abigail had lived here for years peacefully and everyone had turned against her so quickly?

He hoped it wouldn't go any further, but had the sinking suspicion that it would. In a small town, with little else to talk about, someone was always the object of gossip. Never mind if it was factual or not.

His mind kept replaying the morning's events. Something felt off. He wasn't sure what, he just knew that the circumstances didn't sit quite right with him.

While he was trying to be objective, not jump to conclusions, the more he thought about everything, the fact was nothing felt right about the whole situation. That feeling gnawed in his stomach and spun around and around in his mind, almost without stopping.

When school finished for the day, he hurried back to Mrs. Miller's house. He planned to head to Abigail's home, but first wanted to get a book from his room for Sally to practice in.

"Mr. Donner?"

He froze, a hand on his room's doorknob. He'd hoped to avoid this unpleasantness, but fixed a smile on his face and turned around.

"Madam," he greeted Mrs. Miller. "I didn't know you were here."

"It is because I have been in quiet contemplation," she told him, her hands folded before her. "I wish to speak with you."

"Indeed? Should we go to the sitting room?" he asked. That was a preferable location, instead of pressed against his door should she draw closer.

At her nod, Samuel followed her. He observed her every step. Abigail's aunt was acting unusual, even for her. Her face was stern, her demeanor matching. There was an air of unsettledness about her. Was this because of Thomas?

They sat, her perched in the middle of a pale pink horsehair sofa and him in a velvet green plush chair near the window. He waited. She didn't speak. Several moments passed. He could hear the mantel clock ticking.

Just as he was about to clear his throat and ask if another time would be better, Mrs. Miller sighed. "I heard about today, with the Lees boy," she said.

"I see. Yes, it's a strange situation," Samuel said. "I would not have taken Thomas for the destructive type, and I'm still not sure I do."

"I'm sure that the sheriff will figure out what happened," she said with a shrug. "That isn't really what I wanted to talk to you about, though I do wish to caution you about your involvement and defense of the boy."

"Why is that?" Samuel asked.

"Because you are his teacher, and employed by the town. Your position isn't...completely established. Mr. Links has a reputation that all know. You do not."

"Are you saying that if I feel the boy was not in the wrong, and pursue that course, I might find myself no longer the teacher here?"

"That is correct." Mrs. Miller lowered her head briefly, then looked up. "That is why, even though we have little contact, I am keeping my distance from Abigail. I do not wish to be seen as favoring one side of this situation or another. I would advise you to do the same."

Samuel frowned. He realized his hands were clenched into fists. "I am on the side of truth," he told her. "It was a misdeed, done by someone, but I am not convinced the boy is to blame."

She tsked. "It doesn't matter. I've warned you and done my duty. Now, I must tell you something unpleasant, and I'm not sure how to do it, so I simply will."

Unpleasant? Telling him if he supported Abigail or Thomas could compromise his position as teacher wasn't unpleasant? Neither was admitting she wouldn't take any side in the matter? What more could she say?

Samuel waited. Again, there was a long pause. The apprehension about what she might say rose to a nearly unbearable level before Mrs. Miller blurted, "About our marriage."

"Madam—"

"I can't marry you. I'm sorry."

Samuel's mouth slammed shut.

"I didn't want to hurt you, which is why I wasn't brave enough to tell you this before now." She clasped her hands together in front of her. "Oh, Mr. Donner, you are a fine man and a fine teacher. However, you are just too young for me."

"I—"

"No!" She stood, thrusting her hands out to stop him, and then walked to the fireplace, putting one hand on the mantel to hold herself. "Don't protest. I know...I know this is difficult for you. Do you think I don't?" Her face filled with agony. "I am a very empathetic individual. I can feel everything you do."

Samuel stood. "Madam—"

She spun and faced him. "You have to understand, Mr. Donner. A man of your youth. A boy, really. I'm a woman. I need a man. Someone mature. Who knows what he wants in life."

Samuel wondered if he should even open his mouth. It was likely she'd just interrupt him again. He also didn't want to risk her changing her mind. So he kept it clamped shut.

"You make a fine teacher. I'd like you to consider staying. Even if our love is not to be. I know it will be painful for you, but I implore you...think of the children. They must have an education." Mrs. Miller pulled out a handkerchief and dabbed the corners of her eyes. He would have sworn there were real tears. "Say you'll forgive me. Promise you will."

"Madam," Samuel said, then waited. When no interruption came, he continued. "I understand. There is nothing to forgive."

She gave a delighted gasp, and a smile broke over her face. "Then we shall part as friends," she told him, bobbing her head so hard, he watched as her hairpins loosened.

"Indeed," he answered, taking the hand she thrust into his, and giving it a small squeeze before he released it.

"Good," she answered, and started to leave the room. Then, she stopped and looked back at him. "That's why I wanted to warn you, as a friend. Tread carefully with the accusation against the boy."

"Do you know something that I should be aware of?" Samuel asked.

She hesitated. "Only that you are new in town, as I'd said."

Then, she left, and Samuel found himself staring out the window. Mr. Sampson walked past, a satisfied look on his face. The sight stirred something inside of Samuel, and both his dislike and mistrust for the man increased.

No matter what repercussions might be in store, Samuel knew he wouldn't abandon Abigail or Thomas. He knew he was in a difficult spot, but the fact of the matter was, the town needed a teacher. Their decision to keep him on might be influenced by this, yes, but that didn't matter to him. There would always be the need for a teacher of his caliber. He would stand by Abigail, do all he could to help Thomas, and prove that the boy hadn't broken the window or stolen the medal.

He genuinely didn't think that Thomas had done the crime. And he wanted to prove that. To Mr. Links, to the town, and to Abigail.

Abigail.

He felt something for her. There was no denying it. It felt as though she might also be attracted to him. Now that Mrs. Miller had renounced her claim upon him, he felt more confident in telling Abigail how he felt.

There was one problem though, he realized as he started to walk toward her house. With Thomas being accused of a crime, if he were to be seen as too close to Abigail, any good he might be able to do to prove the boy wasn't a criminal might be turned against him, as the townspeople might think he was simply siding with Thomas to pacify or win Abigail. And how would that look, when Mr. Sampson had publicly made it obvious he was pursuing h er?

Here he thought having Mrs. Miller give him up would simplify things. Instead, all of a sudden everything got much more complicated.

Chapter 12

Abigail had not let the children out of her sight since she got them when the school bell rang at dismissal. She pretended she had been passing by. The truth, however, was much different. She didn't trust someone in the town not to make trouble.

They walked home together quietly. Once inside, Thomas had, again, declared his innocence. Abigail believed him—the boy had never done anything destructive or dishonest in his life—but that didn't matter. The opinions of others were what would spread like a wildfire and have consequences.

She planned not to let Thomas out of her sight, nor the other children, and knew she was right to do so.

The following morning, she and the children set out for school. She'd had some misgivings about even letting them go, but was sure she could trust Samuel to keep a close watch on them.

As they drew near, she watched as adults and children started whispering and pointing at her and Thomas.

Some children, adults as well, started calling to them as they neared the general store.

"Thief!" a child called.

"Liar!" another said, throwing a stick.

"Doesn't know how to raise those children," one woman muttered loudly.

"Of course not. They aren't even hers, so what does she care?" another said.

"Turned down a perfectly good man who could have helped her," a man said.

Another didn't answer. He simply spat as they walked past.

Abigail clenched her jaw and, with a firm push on Thomas, Sally, and Little Joe, spun them back toward their house. That's where they stayed the rest of the day. It was difficult to keep an eye on the three of them at once, but they worked in the garden, read inside, and stayed close to one another.

Sally's lip quivered each time she asked why the people had been so mean. Little Jim didn't understand, and just shrugged about the whole thing, but Thomas knew, and he was both angry and hurt, the exact same way that Abigail felt.

When Samuel came by after school, his schoolbooks in his arms, she met him in the yard. Her voice wobbled as she explained what had happened.

"I won't have my child, who did nothing wrong, be attacked." She wiped at an angry tear. "This time was words and a stick. The next time it might be stones or even something done to the house—whether we are inside it or not. This settles it. We cannot stay here. Not in a town like this."

A dark cloud came over his face. Samuel looked as upset as she felt. "How can they think he did that?" he asked. "A boy doesn't break a window to steal something in a frame. He takes money or candy or a toy. I don't even know if he could have reached up that high."

She shrugged. "I don't know. But they do believe it." The hurtful words the women had said about her made her chest tight, and her breath felt hard to squeeze out. Her shoulders sagged, and she admitted, "I never thought we'd be treated like this."

"I will teach the children in the evenings, until things go back to normal," Samuel said. "I won't let them fall behind."

"I'm not even sure if you should continue to come," Abigail said. She bit her lip as she looked at him, then admitted, "I worry you will have others angry at you. You shouldn't risk your job for us."

"It's my duty to teach the children of this town," Samuel said firmly. "I will remind anyone who asks me of that fact." Then, he studied at her, concern in his face. "It is you I worry about. Here, alone."

Abigail smiled and lifted her chin, trying to portray the bravery she didn't feel. "We will be fine. Otherwise, I will deal with it."

It didn't appear that Samuel bought her false confidence, but he nodded. "You'll send one of the children for me if there's anything wrong, won't you?"

She nodded. "Yes. I will."

His face relaxed slightly at that. With a sigh, he stared toward the town, then back at her. "I believe Thomas," he said. "I also will stand by him and by you. I sense there's more to this story than we know."

"Why would there be?" Abigail asked.

"I don't know, but I have my suspicions," Samuel said grimly.

"Let's not speak of them where the children can hear," she said quietly. "It does no good to worry them. They've already had a difficult time since their father died, and I want to make things as trouble-free as possible for them."

He nodded and held up the books. "Can you spare them for lessons?"

"Yes, they'll be glad of the distraction, I'm sure," Abigail said.

They went inside, and though the rest of the evening passed similarly to how it had for the past while, an underlying current of unease filled Abigail. She found herself staring out the window often, wondering when something would happen.

She knew it wasn't a matter of *if* something would happen, but *when*. A surety filled her at the idea she and the children could no longer stay there. The problem, however, she realized as she glanced over at Sally and Little Jim, one on either side of Samuel while he read a story, was that there was one thing she would miss if they did leave. Without a doubt, she'd be leaving behind a piece of her heart. Somewhere along the way, she'd fallen in love with Samuel.

It made her ache inside knowing it could never be. He was kind to her, nothing more. Her feelings of affection were obviously one-sided. As it should be. What was she even doing, thinking about her children's teacher that way?

Abigail shivered and hugged herself tightly. Her thoughts were too dangerous. Longing for what couldn't be never did anyone any good. But as she turned and joined the happy scene before her, Samuel reading and the children wide-eyed with wonder at the tale, she couldn't help but wish, just a little bit.

Chapter 13

"Mr. Donner! Mr. Donner, wait!"

Samuel stopped and turned to see Thomas chasing after him. Abigail was a short distance away, watching with a worried look in her eyes. They'd said goodbye just moments before, after he'd given the children their lesson and joined them for dinner.

The boy was puffing his words out. "Want...talk...you."

"Of course. Did I forget something? Or did you?" Samuel asked. He glanced at Thomas's hands, but they were empty.

"No. I..." The boy gulped a deep breath, as his hands were on his knees, then straightened. "I want to talk to you. Tell you something, but without Ma hearing."

Samuel studied him for a moment. "Of course. You have my undivided attention. I don't think she can hear us from this distance."

"She's gonna watch me until I get back to the house," Thomas said. "She's worried about everything going on."

"I am too," Samuel said. "But you may rest assured that I believe you are telling the truth. You have earned my trust."

"I do." Thomas nodded. "That's what I want to talk to you about."

Samuel's stomach sank. Did that mean Thomas was here to confess to the crime? Before his thoughts could start to spiral, Thomas spoke.

"It wasn't me, but I think it was the man who wants to marry Ma. Mr. Sampson."

Choosing his words carefully, Samuel said, "It's not right to make an accusation against someone without proof to back it up. Merely disliking someone is not grounds for suspicion."

Thomas wrinkled his nose. "I think I understood you, even though you talk pretty fancy sometimes. But I'm not saying I think it's him just because I don't like him."

Truthfully, Samuel wouldn't have blamed him if he did. He felt both a dislike and a mistrust of the man.

"You think all of this is his doing?" Samuel asked. He was sure his eyes narrowed. His body had tensed, and he unclenched his fingers. Samuel wished the sheriff were in town, and hoped he'd hurry back. There was little he wanted to do more than get to the bottom of this.

"He's been here a lot. Doesn't always talk to Ma. Just...wanders around or stands there and looks at the house. Sometimes, when she goes to town, he follows her. I think it might have been him that day following us. Some mornings he did. Always made me feel nervous."

Thomas lowered his eyes, and his toes dug into the ground. Samuel let his eyes follow the boy's bare feet. He knew Abigail was worried about how he needed new shoes. If only there was a way to help her, and her not think it was charity.

"Thank you for telling me," Samuel said. "Any thoughts on what we should do?"

The boy met his eyes. "I'm not sure. But I am worried."

Samuel nodded. "I am too."

"It's just..." Thomas stopped, then shook his head.

"It's what?" Samuel asked gently.

"I wanted you to know because you are newer here. You don't know some things."

"Like what?" Samuel asked.

"Like how Mr. Sampson isn't a nice man. I'm worried if Ma gives in, because she feels like she has to marry him, he might do something bad." Thomas's voice rose slightly.

"Bad in what way?" Samuel asked.

"He's not married anymore, because he hurt his first wife. She ran away," Thomas said, his eyes and face truthful, "and I don't want him to do that to Ma. Hurt her."

Samuel didn't realize he'd sucked in a sharp breath until his chest felt as though it would burst. The man had harmed his first wife? He knew some men did. But he didn't abide by that. Wouldn't allow any woman he was acquainted with to suffer from abuse.

He realized Thomas was watching him. Samuel just hoped that his thoughts right now weren't showing up on his face. He was trying to suppress the rage that was filling him. Setting a good impression was important.

Thomas took in a deep breath, then asked, "You'll help us, Mr. Donner, won't you?"

Samuel's stomach clenched. The boy was looking at him with such trust and hope in his face. What could he say? That he'd do all he could, but that sometimes that wasn't enough? That life was complicated and not always fair? The boy knew that part already.

He didn't want to lie, but he also couldn't give false hope. Samuel reached a hand to Thomas's shoulder and met his eyes. "I promise you I will do all I can for you and your mother. You have my word."

The boy nodded, and started walking backward. In the distance, Samuel could see Abigail still waiting.

"Here," Samuel said, holding out a book. "In case you need an excuse for why you ran after me. And so you have something to read tomorrow between chores."

Thomas took it with a grin. "I like you being here," he said. "You're okay, Mr. Donner."

Then, he spun around and ran back to Abigail, who led him into the house. He saw her smile at him, though, and Samuel raised a hand in farewell.

"You're okay too, kid," he said, though he knew Thomas wouldn't be able to hear him. "And so's your mother."

Thunder sounded in the distance, and dark clouds started to fill the sky. Samuel hurried to get back to his room at Mrs. Miller's house before the books he was holding got damp.

Just as the first fat raindrops fell, he reached the front door. Samuel let himself in. The house was quiet. She must have been out somewhere. He went to his room and stared out the window. This entire thing about Thomas and the theft, and Mr. Sampson pursuing Abigail was troubling him.

Opening one of his notebooks to a fresh page, he carefully wrote down all he knew about Thomas, Mr. Sampson, and the theft. Then, he wrote down what the boy had told him the day of the theft and just now. After reading it over, he shook his head. It still didn't make sense. No clues or any missing piece of information stood out to him. The only thing that was clear was Mr. Sampson seemed obsessed with Abigail, and that could be dangerous.

With a sigh, he closed the book and spent the next hour reading over the school children's homework. He had a bright group of students, and it made him proud to see just how well they were flourishing under his tutelage.

Every now and then, he watched the storm outside. The rain had picked up, and in the distance lightning flashed. Samuel had always enjoyed watching a storm occur and pass. As a child, when it wasn't windy, his mother would let him sit on their covered porch in a blanket and watch the sky. He liked the sound of the rain and the show nature provided.

Did Abigail? Would she want to watch with him?

As soon as he wondered that, he shook himself. That wasn't appropriate for him to wonder. She was the mother of his students. Nothing more.

Except...for that she wasn't. And somewhere along the way of knowing her, he'd realized he cared deeply for her. This was a new thing for him. He'd always held his emotions tightly in check. Letting them slip through the crack she'd made was almost confusing at how easy and how right it all felt.

He wanted to see her happy, to see her with that peaceful expression she so seldom wore. He wanted to see the worry leave her face. To have it replaced with laughter.

Samuel swallowed. He hadn't expected that at all. A wife was not why he'd come to Cottonwood Falls. In fact, the very idea of one had originally made him consider leaving.

But that was before he met Abigail. Abigail was different. He knew that. Could feel it deep within him.

Abigail felt as though she…was perfect for him. The idea terrified Samuel. But the image of her inside of his mind being wed to Mr. Sampson was worse.

He didn't know what to do, and felt helpless. Mrs. Miller's warning to him about siding with Abigail played in his mind. Would the townspeople really treat him poorly? Or was the brunt of their anger going to be put on Abigail? What might they do? He wasn't sure, but he intended to ask Abigail the next time he saw her if she'd had any difficulties with those in town. Surely, there had to be something he could do. Sitting here, worrying but being unable to act, was killing him inside.

Samuel didn't know when he'd become so involved with wanting to care for Abigail and her children, but he had, and now it felt too late to back away. Even if he did, he'd never forget just how much he cared for her.

A crack of thunder jolted him, but it seemed to awaken some sort of resolve. "I'll do what I must," he said quietly. As he watched the storm, Samuel knew whatever it took to protect her, he would do. *Even if she doesn't care for me the way I do her, I will keep her safe.*

Chapter 14

A soft bell jangled over the bakery door, and Abigail hesitantly walked inside. It had been a difficult morning. She'd left the children inside the house, telling them to lock the door and stay away from the windows.

Then, she'd hurried into town with a basket full of eggs and butter. It was a necessity, and the reason she'd dared risk them alone. Only, when she arrived at the bakery, she wasn't met with a smile.

"We don't need your eggs or butter," the baker's wife said. She turned away and greeted the woman who entered behind her, chattering away and serving her. When the customer left, Abigail watched as the baker's wife left without a word, heading into the kitchen.

Abigail stood there for a moment, almost frozen in shock. Then, the realization as to why the woman had refused her offering and ignored her struck her. They didn't think she was a trustworthy person, and wouldn't allow her to trade.

She swallowed hard and tried to stifle the embarrassment that started to fill her. It had been an absolute blessing that there had not been anyone else there at the time it happened, and that the customer had entered a moment later. Abigail was sure she wouldn't be able to handle that mortification.

Once outside, Abigail hesitated. Where else could she try? They needed flour. Wheat would do, if she couldn't get anything else. She could grind it if need be, but they needed something. There was so little left, she wasn't able to make but a small loaf. That wouldn't even be enough for the day. No flour meant no bread and no biscuits, or most anything else.

Her eyes landed on the general store. There was simply nowhere else to go. No one else in town sold flour. Her steps were slow and heavy as she crossed to the store. She stopped outside of the door and looked at it for a long moment.

Abigail didn't want to go inside. The only reason she was there after Mr. Links had accused her son of theft was desperation. They simply had more eggs and butter than needed, and very little flour. Bread must be made. It filled small bellies.

She pushed open the door, and hesitantly crossed the store, focusing on putting one foot in front of the other. Luckily, the store was empty, as had been the bakery. There was no one to see her shame and how she was near begging.

"Good morning," Abigail said, her throat feeling tight. "I need some flour. I-I have two dozen eggs and a quart of butter."

Mr. Links pressed his lips together as she set the basket on the counter. "Don't need the eggs or butter," he told her. "But I'll sell you the flour."

Abigail's heart was hammering, but she nodded. What else could she do? As he scooped the flour into a small bag, perhaps enough for three loaves, she reached into her coin purse, tried not to grimace at the few coins there, and pulled out the usual amount.

"That's not enough," Mr. Links said, setting the flour down. "Price has gone up."

A roaring sound filled Abigail's ears as he told her how much. "But...but that's almost triple what I paid last time," she gasped.

"Got a broken window to pay for," Mr. Links said. "Only right the thief's mother pays for it. That doesn't even take care of the problem of the missing medal."

"Thomas didn't break the window or steal your medal," Abigail said. She looked at him, hoping her panic didn't come through the tears blurring her vision, and said, "I thought that we were waiting for the sheriff to return and investigate before accusing anyone of anything."

He crossed his arms and didn't say anything. Abigail sucked in a breath and straightened her shoulders. "Never mind. I won't be needing that flour after all. Thank you, Mr. Links. Good afternoon."

She turned, and stopped short as she found herself face to face with Mr. Sampson. His balding scalp was red and flaky, and as he scratched at it, her stomach churned.

"Well, hello there," he said, and tucked his thumbs into his pant pockets. "A little short on money? I'll buy what you need. You can pay me back later."

"No thank you," she said stiffly. "We are fine."

"That's not what I hear," Mr. Sampson said, and he reached for her arm. Abigail sidestepped him.

"I don't know what you hear," she said, keenly aware that Mr. Links was listening to the conversation, likely his eyes were riveted on the interaction, "but I doubt it's true."

"You know," Mr. Sampson said. "Things would be so much better for you if you just married me. Think about it. You wouldn't want for nothing."

But love. The word was in her mind before Abigail could even blink. She frowned and shook her head. Love didn't buy food for the children or put shoes on their feet, but even still, she'd figure out something before she gave in to Mr. Sampson's advances.

"I've told you no," she said.

"You're stubborn," he said, his voice low and hard. "I like a woman who tries to get away from me. Makes it more fun."

Something about his words chilled Abigail all the way through. She tried to step past, but he grabbed her arm again and squeezed. "Really like it," he added.

"Let me go," Abigail demanded, her voice cold. "I don't know how many times I have to tell you. I won't marry you. I also won't sell you the property."

"You will," he answered. "You'll see."

She twisted away from him and stormed out, aware of two sets of eyes watching her.

Anger burned in her all the way back to her house, erasing all traces of the embarrassment she'd felt only a short time earlier. Once there, she put the eggs and the butter away, ignoring the children asking if she was all right. A glance into a sack showed there was plenty of cornmeal, so cornbread it would be for a while. Perhaps she could hitch up the wagon and head to Spring Falls and buy the flour from their general store.

She set the children to shelling peas and went out to the barn. On the way there, a sob wrenched free, and then another. It was too much. It was all too much.

Her arm still ached from where Mr. Sampson had grabbed it. When she pushed up her sleeve, Abigail could see a bruise in the shape of his fingers forming. There had been rumors he'd treated his first wife badly. It seemed it was true. She shuddered as she recalled the look in his eyes. Predatory. That's what.

Abigail reached into her dress pocket and pulled out the slip of paper she'd been carrying around all day. She read it to herself once more.

Wanted. A husband who is kind and willing to accept me and help provide for the children that belonged to my first husband. They have no one else, and I promised to love and care for them as my own. I will do the same for any man who might have his own children. I cook well, am educated, can grow a garden, and hope one day to find love in our marriage.

Was that enough to help her find a husband? Was there more she should say? An old newspaper that she'd found in the barn had the address of a mail-order agency, and she'd begun her letter to them. As she'd never done that before, Abigail wasn't quite sure what to say. Once she mailed the letter, she hoped to hear something back soon.

Trying to block out her troubling thoughts, she went through the barn chores. Abigail grabbed the three-legged stool to sit on for a moment, but as soon as she sat on it, a leg snapped, sending her sprawling on the ground.

What more? The day had been a disaster, and it wasn't even noon. Her backside ached. Her heart ached. Tears fell down her cheeks, and sobs shook her so violently her head pounded. What was she to do? That single question spun over and over again in her mind, but she just didn't know.

"Oh, Jim," she whispered. "Why'd you leave us? I can't do this on my own."

Chapter 15

Samuel stepped back a little after he knocked at the door. He wanted to be sure Abigail and the kids could see him clearly so they knew who was at the door. Sally opened it wide. Her face was serious, which was unusual. Sally always smiled.

"Mr. Donner," she said. "Are you here for lessons?"

"I am," he told her. "Where's your mother? Does she need help with something first?"

"Ma's crying in the barn," Little Jim said, looking up from a slate he was copying letters on. "She thinks we don't know."

"Why is she crying?" Samuel asked, trying not to let his fears jump to conclusions. Had something happened to her? Was she hurt? Sick?

Thomas took the books Samuel was holding and carried them to the table. "I think it's because no one would buy the eggs or butter. She didn't come back from the store with flour or anything, so I guess maybe they wouldn't sell it to her. Because of me." He lowered his head.

"It wasn't anything you did," Samuel said firmly, and put his hand on the boy's shoulder. He squeezed it, and then faced the children. "Sometimes, adults act just as badly as undisciplined children."

Sally giggled at that. "Really?"

"Yes," he told her firmly, tugging on one of her braided pigtails. "Now, can I trust you children to start your math problems while I check on your mother?"

At their nods, he made sure the front door was locked, and went out the back door, the one closest to the barn. Samuel's long legs strode across to the barn. He walked inside, and didn't see Abigail.

He was about to call for her when he saw the broken stool, and a short distance away, her, lying there in a heap.

"Abigail," he gasped and rushed over.

She tried to wave him away. "I'm fine," she said. "It broke when I tried to sit."

He went onto his knees, helping her to sit, and studied her face. Her eyes were red, and her face blotchy. It was as Little Jim had said, she'd been crying. Bits of straw had buried themselves in her hair, and long strands had come loose from the low bun she'd been wearing.

Samuel carefully picked the straw from her hair, and gently asked, "What happened?"

"It's old, and worn out." She shrugged, wiping the back of her hand across her eyes. "Like me, I guess. It was bound to break." Then she softly added, "Same as me."

"Not the stool," Samuel said, and moved closer to her. "Who cares about that? It's you I'm worried about. What's happened?"

She shook her head, but he could see her swallowing. A sob broke free, and she dropped her head into her hands.

Samuel didn't wait. He took Abigail into his arms. He knew he shouldn't, but he didn't care what others might say. It was comfort she needed, and he, selfishly, didn't want anyone else to give it but him.

Abigail didn't stiffen, didn't protest, but rested her head on his chest and let her tears flow. Samuel's heart was breaking for her. He had no idea what to do, but he held her tightly, one hand on the back of her head stroking her hair, the other on her back, moving in a slow circle.

"Tell me what happened," he said quietly.

As Abigail told him, between sobs, of her humiliation at being rejected at the bakery, and then how Mr. Links had tripled his price, Samuel found himself getting angry. When she told him how Mr. Sampson had made his disgusting comments toward her, he had to make a conscious effort to not squeeze her tightly in his fury, as his muscles tensed of their own accord.

Instead, he focused on her in his arms. The sweet smell of her hair, and the soothing motions he was making on her back. She kept him grounded. In truth, Samuel wasn't one to lose his temper, not really. However, the last few days had caused a swift change in that.

What he felt, he decided, wasn't anger just to be angry, but a sort of righteous indignation. How dare they treat Abigail this way? Even her own aunt, who, granted, never spent much effort or time on her before, was ignoring her out of fear of some sort of retribution.

"I'll get the flour," he said. "Whatever else you need as well."

"No," she said, shaking her head and pulling back slightly. "Not another cent of my money will go to someone who refuses to believe me. I'll hitch the wagon and go to Spring Falls. It's a long drive, but worth it."

"Tell me when, and I'll go with you," Samuel promised. "We'll make—" he almost said *make a family day of it*, but then remembered he wasn't part of the family. "Make a day of it," he finished.

Family. When had that come into his mind? What had made him think, feel, for a moment that she and the children were his?

Samuel wasn't sure, but it felt correct in thinking. He brushed a strand of hair back from Abigail's face. She met his eyes and smiled. "Thank you," she said softly. "I really am so glad you are here."

"I am too," he said. "I'm here for as long as you want me."

Abigail shook her head. "I've no right to ask or expect that. But I appreciate it, appreciate you. I won't lie, Samuel. I'm scared. Worst of all, I have no idea what to do, or where to go."

She reached into her pocket and pulled out a folded, slightly crumpled paper. "I even wrote this. To send to a mail-order agency."

A wave of nausea washed over Samuel. He knew she'd mentioned such a possibility, but had things gotten so desperate? As soon as he thought that, he berated himself. Of course they had. No one would sell to her or take her eggs and butter. She had children to provide for. And here he wasn't doing anything to help her. Not really.

Though his stomach was churning and his heart was pounding, Samuel forced himself to try to say what he'd been thinking. "Abigail, you don't need to be a mail-order bride." As she started to protest, he hurried on, "You don't need a mail-order husband. You already have one."

Her look was one of puzzlement. "I'm not sure what you mean."

There was a buzzing sound in his ears, and Samuel wondered when he'd grown to be such a coward. He forced the words out. "Me. Me, Abigail. Remember? Your aunt sent away for a mail-order husband for you. Thank goodness, she doesn't want me, but...I could be your husband. If you wanted me."

"Oh, Samuel," Abigail said. She shook her head. "I don't want you feeling forced or obligated or anything else."

"I'm not," he said, then added, before she could say anything else, "I promise I'll take care of you. If we are married, that's much easier for me to do."

Abigail opened her mouth to protest. Or to deny him. He wasn't sure which. All Samuel knew was he was desperate to finish what he had to say before he couldn't.

He continued, "Your happiness means so much to me. Your smiles are something I look forward to, your laughter makes me happy. Being around you, I feel complete."

Samuel wasn't sure what the look on her face was, but she hadn't pulled away, so he was hoping that was a good sign. Samuel reached for her hands.

It was too late to take back any of what he said, so Samuel just waited, hoped she would say something.

"Samuel," she whispered, and his name on her lips had never sounded so sweet.

He released one of her hands to bring his to her cheek. Her skin was so soft, and she leaned into his palm. Samuel inched closer. Abigail did the same.

Was now the time to tell her? To use the actual words? *Abigail, I love you.* Or should he kiss her? Samuel wasn't sure. He inched closer, hardly daring to breathe. Abigail looked as nervous as he felt, but she moved closer, and

Samuel had just decided he'd kiss first, then tell her how he felt, when the sound of someone shouting in the yard startled them and destroyed the moment.

"Mrs. Lees? My deputy and I are here for your boy."

Chapter 16

Abigail froze, then she scrambled to her feet. Her heart was pounding. She wasn't entirely sure if that was because Samuel had practically proposed to her and, for a moment, she thought he might kiss her, or if it was because the sheriff was there.

The children rushed to her, but she urged them back inside, keeping only Thomas by her side, since it was obvious the sheriff would want to talk to him. Samuel stood nearby, his expression one of calm. She found strength in that.

"Sheriff, Deputy," Abigail said politely. She felt proud her voice didn't wobble from fear or anger. Both were warring inside of her for domination.

"Ma'am," the sheriff said. "We've come to talk to your boy, and to bring him in to the office."

"Why?" Abigail asked, putting an arm around Thomas.

"Mr. Links explained to us what happened. There was also another crime done today, again at the general store." The deputy looked uncomfortable. "I'm sorry, but the boy has been accused, and we need to get to the bottom of this."

Abigail opened her mouth to protest when Samuel spoke. "When was this other theft?" he asked. "The boy has been staying home, assisting his mother for the last few days."

"About a half hour ago," the sheriff said.

"But that can't be," Abigail said. She looked between the men. "Thomas has been here."

"That's right," Samuel agreed. "I can attest to that fact. I've been coming to give the children their lessons. Thomas was here when I arrived, which was a little over an hour ago. He's been working on his math and history lessons this afternoon."

The sheriff and his deputy exchanged glances. "Begging your pardon for suggesting it, Mr. Donner," the sheriff said, "but we were told you might side with Mrs. Lees."

"I'm not siding with anyone," Samuel said. "I'm siding with the truth. You are welcome to look at the children's copy work as proof." He hesitated. "Do you mind telling who accused him?"

"Mr. Links, of course," the deputy answered. "Was his property damaged."

"And did Mr. Links see Thomas?" Abigail asked.

"Well, no," the deputy said. "But we have another witness who did."

"Was it Mr. Sampson?" Abigail asked softly.

The sheriff nodded.

"Thomas, go inside the house," Abigail said. "Read to your brother and sister."

She waited until Thomas was inside the house, then said, "Sheriff, I don't know how to say this without sounding blunt, but I believe Mr. Sampson is making up accusations because I am refusing his offer of marriage, and his offer to buy this land."

"Now, I don't know why he'd do such a thing," the deputy protested, but the sheriff put a hand out, and the man quieted.

"Why do you think that?" he asked.

"Actually, Sheriff," Samuel said, "I've been waiting for you to get back. I have some information that...well, Abigail, I hadn't told you because I didn't want to worry you."

She looked at him in surprise, then gave a bitter laugh. "I doubt I could worry more than I do."

Samuel sighed, then looked at the sheriff. "It's my understanding Mr. Sampson has been watching Abigail, following her, and lurking about her property."

Abigail swallowed hard. Her mouth felt dry. The man always was underfoot. How had she never realized it?

What kind of danger had she been in? Her encounter with the man inside the general store replayed itself. "He...has not been accepting of my refusal to marry him," she said, her voice low. "In front of Mr. Links, he told me that...he insinuated..."

She couldn't. Humiliation washed over her, and Abigail's cheeks flushed. She started to shake and wrapped her arms around herself.

Samuel stepped closer. "You need to tell them, so they can help you." He looked at the sheriff. "You also should ask Mr. Links if he overheard. It would be proof."

She nodded. He was right. Her voice just above a whisper, she said, "When I told him no again today, he grabbed my arm and squeezed it tightly." She pushed up her dress sleeve and showed the bruising. The sheriff frowned, and she heard Samuel's breath hitch.

"He told me he liked it when women ran. It was fun for him. When I tried to pull away again, he squeezed even harder and said he really liked it. Once more, I told him I wouldn't marry him, and he said yes, I would." Abigail bit her lip. "I'm not wanting any trouble, Sheriff. I just want to take care of my children. Thomas didn't do anything wrong. Of that, I'm sure."

There was a long silence. The deputy was rubbing at his jaw, the sheriff looking back toward the town.

Samuel said, "I have heard that the first Mrs. Sampson was...treated poorly."

"It's true," the sheriff said. "I locked him up a few times for hurting her. I thought, though..."

"I won't marry him," Abigail whispered. "But if he's going to be a threat to me and my children, I will leave to protect them. And until that moment arrives, I will do what I must to keep them safe."

"I'm sure it won't come to that," the sheriff said.

"What was damaged?" Samuel asked suddenly.

"Back window, the one that was just replaced," the deputy answered.

"There's nothing back there, though," Samuel said. "Why would a child damage such a spot?"

"I don't know," the sheriff mused. His eyes were sharp as he looked at her and Samuel. "Because he could?"

"Boys who are looking to get into trouble want something to show for it," Samuel said, shaking his head. "That's one thing I've learned in my years of teaching." Then he asked, "Did you ever get into any trouble, Sheriff?"

The sheriff and the deputy glanced at each other and grinned. Samuel laughed, then shared. "I remember once, I thought I was so clever. I snuck into the kitchen and helped myself to the cookie jar. Didn't realize I'd left a trail of crumbs. They followed me all the way back to my room, where I sat there, happy as can be, eating, when my mother found me. I couldn't sit for the rest of the day."

The men laughed, and the sheriff nodded. "I did the same." He got a thoughtful look on his face. "I see your point. Young boys are clever, but not usually clever enough to hide their tracks. I also happen to agree with you. However, facts are, the boy's been accused, and I needed to come see for myself. I'd like to talk with him, get his side," the sheriff said.

Abigail hesitated, but then nodded and went to the house and called for Thomas. She stood quietly as the sheriff and his deputy asked Thomas a good number of questions. Samuel was close by, but stayed silent. At one point, he gently put a hand on her lower back before he removed it.

The touch was unnerving. It filled Abigail with shivers, and she wanted to move closer, to take every ounce of strength and distraction Samuel could provide. But that was dangerous. She needed to focus, to take care of the children.

The entire situation, since Samuel had come to town, had been distracting. *He* was distracting. There were moments Abigail didn't know how or what to think. Then, there were others when all she could do was daydream.

The sheriff walked over to her. "Thank you, Mrs. Lees. We're done here. Thomas will stay, for now. If I have any more questions, I'll let you know. I do plan to take your suggestion, Mr. Donner, and ask Mr. Links about what he overheard."

She nodded.

Samuel said, "I'm going to walk back with the sheriff, join them on their visit if that's not a problem. I'll come by again tomorrow."

Abigail nodded. "Of course. Thank you."

She watched as the men left, then turned back to the house. As she walked inside, Thomas asked, "Is it time for the milking?"

"Oh goodness," Abigail said. "Yes. But you stay here, I'll go."

"I can do it," he offered.

"Yes, but I want you here, safe."

He sighed. "Yes, Ma."

She smiled at him and dropped a kiss on the top of his head. "It's just for a little longer." Abigail grabbed the milk pail and headed toward the barn. Luckily, though the one stool had broken, she knew there was a wooden crate she could sit on to do the milking.

Bessie the cow was crying out as she walked in. "I'm hurrying," Abigail laughed as she increased her step.

Then she stopped. Two figures stepped out from the shadows. One was Mr. Sampson, the other a man she'd never seen before, holding a long knife. The bucket clattered from her fingers, and as the person with the knife lunged at her, Abigail screamed and ran toward the house.

The person grabbed her arm, spinning her around. Abigail screamed again, hoping that Samuel and the sheriff weren't so far away that they couldn't hear her.

Her cry for help stopped as the person backhanded her, and she felt her teeth rattle. Abigail crumpled to the ground, but tried to stand. She had to get up. Had to protect the children.

"I told you, you're going to marry me," Mr. Sampson snarled, moving closer. "Me. Not the teacher, me. I saw his hand on you! You'll regret that. You are mine."

"I'm not marrying anyone," Abigail said defiantly. "Especially not you." His foot connected with her stomach, and she gasped at the jolt of pain it caused.

"You will," he corrected, pulling her upward by twisting her arm.

Abigail's vision dimmed from the pain. It was taking everything within her to stay alert, to try and focus. His voice sounded far away, and she felt herself be released, but only for a moment. A new kind of hurting filled her as he gripped her hair close to her scalp.

"I know all the ways to make you agree," he said, leaning close, his foul breath spitting droplets on her. "You want those brats safe? You do as I say. Every time."

"I will never," Abigail said. She brought her foot up and stomped as hard as she could on his ankle.

With a yelp of surprise, Mr. Sampson released his grip on her. Abigail ran, almost making it out of the barn, and screamed. "Get help! Run! Get to town!"

The last word was cut off again, as she was grabbed from behind, and the knife slashed out at her. Her arm burned from the pain and blood soaked her dress sleeve.

"Grab her, hurry up," Mr. Sampson spat to the other man.

Abigail twisted as two arms clamped around her, one on her mouth, the other around her arms, and she was dragged backward. She was captured, and now unable to see even a portion of the house. She had no idea if the children knew what was happening, if they could get help, or even if they would be Mr. Sampson's next victims.

Chapter 17

"I understand your concerns, Mr. Donner," the sheriff sighed. "But I'm not in an easy position. Mr. Links is a respected member of the town. He holds a lot of sway."

"I understand," Samuel said. "And I—"

"Help! Help us!"

Samuel turned sharply. The sheriff and deputy did as well, their hands on their guns. Sally was streaking toward them as fast as she could, fear on her face.

Without thinking, Samuel ran toward her. "What's happened?"

"There's men! They grabbed Ma! She's bleeding and screaming!"

The sheriff took off, the deputy right behind him. Samuel grabbed Sally. "Get the doctor. Tell him to send more help, and his doctor's bag," he ordered her. "Run and do not stop and do not look back."

She nodded and ran, her small legs carrying her as quickly as they could. Samuel bolted toward Abigail's house, and saw a small heap on the ground.

Thomas didn't look as though he were breathing. The deputy kneeled next to him. Samuel feared for the worst. Thankfully, as he approached, there was movement from the boy.

"I couldn't stop them," Thomas groaned. "They came after her right as she went to do the milking. I followed when I saw, but..." He groaned again. There was a bruise forming on his face. Samuel felt angrier than he ever had. What adult would strike a child?

"That's all right, son. We're here," the deputy said. "Where are they now? Did they take her away?"

"In the barn," Thomas said.

As the sheriff and his deputy split up, taking opposite sides of the barn, Samuel helped Thomas to his feet. "I'm going too. Get in the house."

"Have to help," Thomas mumbled, clearly disoriented. He wobbled as he tried to step forward. "I'm man of the house."

"You've got to protect your brother," Samuel said. "That's your job. The sheriff is here to protect your mother."

Thomas nodded, and stumbled to the door. He was let in, the door latched behind him, and Samuel slipped to the side of the barn where the sheriff was.

"Come out. We know you've got Mrs. Lees. You let her go and come on with me. Hands up where I can see them," the sheriff called.

There were voices, angry, but not directed toward the sheriff. Instead, it seemed like the men, whoever they were, were having some sort of an argument.

"Not going to do this. Not worth it. You're on your own," a voice said.

"I paid you," another snapped. "You'll finish the job. I can't carry her. You get her to my place. I'll pay extra."

"Forget it," the first said. "Ain't worth being killed. You didn't say nothing about there being kids and the sheriff. I don't hurt kids, and I ain't going to jail."

The argument continued. The sheriff shook his head. "I don't know the first man's voice, but the other is Sampson. That I recognize."

Samuel spoke quietly. "I hope this will be proof enough that what Abigail said is the truth? Perhaps even what Thomas said was the truth."

"One thing at a time, Mr. Donner," the sheriff said. "Let's get her out of there safely."

The sheriff was scanning the barn. He was at one exit along the side for cover; the deputy was at the other. The problem was they didn't know if the men inside were armed. It was likely. The other thing they didn't know was how frightened or how desperate the men were.

If they were feeling backed into a corner, with nothing to lose, who would be their target? The sheriff and his deputy? Or Abigail? Thankfully, the boys were inside of the house, and Sally in town, but Samuel knew they had to be terrified. He was.

"I should have never left," he said. "I knew Thomas said Mr. Sampson had been hanging around. I should have stayed in case he was nearby."

"Wasn't your place to do so," the sheriff said. "Was mine. I fully intended to set up a watch. Too late now."

It wasn't his place. No. But Samuel wanted it to be. He decided until this was over, he wouldn't be leaving Abigail. Like it or not, he'd stay here to watch over her. Even if that meant he had to sleep outside.

There was the sound of a scuffle and a shot was fired inside the barn. Abigail shrieked, then stopped suddenly. Samuel lunged to go in, but the sheriff pulled him back.

"Wait. It could be a trick," the sheriff warned, his voice low. "Trying to draw us out."

Just then, a horse streaked from the far side of the barn, a man low on his back. The deputy fired and missed. He chased after him a few paces, then turned around, settling back by the barn.

"Don't worry, we'll get him," the sheriff assured Samuel, never taking his eyes off a crack of the barn's wall he was peering through. "Mrs. Lees first, though."

The sheriff pulled back, slipped alongside of the barn, whispered for a few moments to the deputy, then returned. He held up three fingers, then dropped them. He raised his hand once more, and nodded at the interior of the barn. Samuel understood then. The sheriff and his deputy planned to enter the opposite sides of the barn at the same time. If it was just Sampson, he'd be distracted and unable to shoot at both men at once.

The odds weren't the best, but he knew the man wanted Abigail alive, and was unlikely to kill her. Especially in front of witnesses.

Samuel took a deep breath. He was prepared to go in as well. He might not have a weapon, but he wasn't abandoning Abigail. Not when she needed him most.

The sheriff held up three fingers. Two fingers...

Chapter 18

"Get up," Mr. Sampson hissed.

As she struggled to her knees, Abigail winced. Her whole body hurt, especially her arm. Where the blood had started to dry made the fabric of her dress stiff, and it pulled at her skin, reopening the wound.

Mr. Sampson was pacing. When the man with the gun—she still didn't know his name—had raced from the barn, she'd felt a moment of relief. Now, that was gone and panic had returned.

The sheriff had called he was outside, but that didn't matter. She wasn't convinced the man would help her. Not when he suspected Thomas of vandalism. Her thoughts turned to the children, and her eyes followed.

A slow smile formed on Mr. Sampson's face. "I know just what you are thinking. Worrying about those children. I promise I'll keep them safe, even might let you keep them, if you do what I say."

She wasn't sure what to do. To refuse him again and risk his anger, or buy time. Abigail chose to be quiet.

He walked closer to her. His eyes were hard, his sneer cold. "I told you that you'd marry me. Hadn't realized you'd be this much trouble. I can make a lot more for you and your oldest." He dug into his pocket and pulled out a medal. "The town thinks he's the crook. I'll be a hero, not just for returning the medal, but also marrying the mother of the criminal to rehabilitate him."

"It was you?" Abigail gasped. "You broke the window? Stole the medal?"

He laughed. "Sure did. Now. We're going to leave. Get on my horse. The reverend will marry us, and then you'll be mine." He laughed, and the sound sent chills down her spine. "Going to be real fun once we are."

"Step away," the sheriff said, showing himself.

"Put your hands up," the deputy ordered from behind her.

Mr. Sampson spun, then twisted back and forth, unsure who to look at. He grabbed Abigail's bleeding arm and twisted it once more. Tears came to her eyes, and she felt weak from the pain. Her body wanted to collapse from it, but she tried to move enough to take the pressure off her shoulder before he broke her arm.

"Get away from her," Samuel said. He walked closer, ignoring the sheriff telling him to get back.

"You're going to tell me what to do?" Mr. Sampson sneered. "You're a sissy. A prissy city boy." He laughed. "What are you going to do to me?"

"Let her go, and I'll show you," Samuel said. He shrugged. "Or are you afraid to fight me, man to man? Only want to hurt those who can't fight back."

"Oh, that hellcat fought back," he snarled. "And she'll get punished for it later." He pushed Abigail to the side. She stumbled, and caught herself on the barn wall.

"Put 'em up," Mr. Sampson laughed.

Quicker than Abigail could draw her breath, Samuel had done just so. He raised his fists, then punched Mr. Sampson right in the jaw. The man stood for a second, shock on his face before his eyes rolled back and he fell backward onto the ground.

The sheriff's mouth fell open, and Abigail stared in surprise at Samuel. "Where...did you learn to do that?"

He grinned proudly. "Captain of my school's boxing class," he told her. Then, he put his hands on her face, scrutinizing her. "You're bleeding. Where is it coming from?"

"My arm, mostly," she told him.

"Sally has gone for the doctor. He'll be here soon," he told her, and helped her to sit.

The sheriff and his deputy were tying up Mr. Sampson. She watched as they made sure the rope knots were tight.

"He has the medal," she said suddenly. "From Mr. Links."

"Heard the whole thing," the sheriff said.

"But what of the other man?" Abigail asked, then hissed in pain as Samuel touched a cut near her eye.

"We'll find him," the sheriff said. "I'm going to make a posse. You recognize him?"

She shook her head. Suddenly, she felt so tired. So weak.

"Let me get you to the house," Samuel said, and picked her up effortlessly.

Abigail wanted to protest, but couldn't. Her body ached, and she wanted to see the children and make sure they were okay. Her head rested against Samuel's chest. A small smile came as she remembered his pleased expression at hitting Mr. Sampson.

As if he knew what she was thinking, he chuckled. "I've been wanting to deck that man since the moment I first heard him talking about you."

She laughed softly. "I don't feel the least bit bad that you did."

"Neither do I."

They got to the house, and Thomas had the door open. Samuel set her down gently at the kitchen table.

"Thomas, we're going to need water. Get me plenty, and put some on the stove," Samuel directed.

"It's not safe out there," Abigail said, trying to stand.

"The sheriff hasn't left yet. It'll be okay," Samuel told her. "But I'll fetch the water. You sit."

He was back in a moment, Sally and the doctor right behind him.

"Ma!" Sally shrieked. She tried to run to her, but Samuel caught her.

"Let the doctor take a look first," he said.

Abigail sat still while Dr. Edward Mason examined her, then set to cleaning the cuts on her face and the larger wound on her arm. The pain was incredible as he washed her arm, and then put a salve on it before he wrapped it. She wondered if she was delirious, as she sat there trying to figure out how she could save her blood-stained and torn dress. There was no money to replace it.

"Rest is what you need," the doctor said sternly. "If you need anything, if the pain in your arm increases, send for me right away. If I am away on a call, my wife Caroline will come. She's as competent as they come."

She nodded. "Thank you, Doctor."

"Thank you," Samuel repeated, and walked him outside. When he returned, he said, "The sheriff and the deputy have just hauled Mr. Sampson off and are forming the posse now." He hesitated, then said, "Proper or not, I'm staying here until the other man is caught. I can sleep outside, or in a chair, but I won't leave you and the children alone."

Abigail wanted to protest, but there was no point. She could tell by the look in his eye.

"Now then," Samuel said. "Let me figure out what to do for dinner while you rest."

Abigail was so tired she didn't want to argue. An hour later, when she woke, she was relieved to note she felt refreshed. There was also a wonderful smell. Abigail walked into the kitchen area and glanced around. "Where are the children?" she asked.

"With the kitten," Samuel said. "In the loft. They aren't outside."

"Kitten?" Abigail asked.

"Yes. A short time ago, Caroline, the doctor's wife, stopped by with this meal and a kitten. She thought it might be a comfort to the children, after the stress of today."

Abigail shook her head, but smiled. "And now, that's one more thing I'll have to hope is allowed when we leave."

"Are you...still thinking about that?" Samuel asked. "Leaving?" He set a covered dish on the table.

"Even with Mr. Sampson caught, and what he's done brought to light, I'm still in a terrible way," Abigail confessed with a sigh, "with more to do than I am capable of, and no money to provide with."

He was quiet, then said, "I apologize. For earlier. If I put any sort of pressure upon you, to think about a marriage with me."

"You didn't," Abigail said. She moved closer to him. "I just...I don't want you to be hasty. To choose me because you feel sorry for me. That's not what you deserve."

Samuel's jaw clenched for a moment, then he said, "That's not why I said what I did. I don't want to be yet another man pressuring you to do something you have no interest in. Maybe it was fate that I arrived, I'm not sure, but I don't want to be with you out of pity or kindness or anything else, but because I like you. It's okay if you don't feel the same. I understand."

Abigail's breath caught. "You like me?"

"I do," he said, bringing a hand to her face. He dropped it again. "My feelings for you are deeper than anything I can think of. I want you to be part of my every day. That is...if you want me. I hope you might want me. Could love me. I already know that I love you."

Abigail wasn't sure what to say, not wanting to confuse her gratitude with love, if that's not what it was. It was true, something had been building. An affection of some kind. Longing and wondering about the what ifs. But, despite his words, she wasn't sure how to answer.

The children burst into the kitchen just then, a tiny black kitten in hand. The words Abigail was going to say were kept locked inside as the children surrounded her, and then Samuel ushered them all to the table for a meal.

Over the hearty chicken and dumplings, Abigail lost herself once again in the happiness at the table. It was as though what had happened earlier was a dream, and only the pain in her arm contradicted her.

Samuel's warm eyes met hers every now and then, and she felt torn. She needed to think. If she were to say yes, it was not just her life affected, but three others as well. He would need an answer soon. What was she to say?

Chapter 19

"Here, let me get that." Samuel hoisted the two buckets of water and carried them to the house.

"Thank you," Abigail said. "You've been such a tremendous help to me. I'm so grateful."

"I'm actually really enjoying myself," Samuel said, as he gave her a grin. "I've never worked in a garden before, or milked a cow, or anything else like this before arriving to Cottonwood Falls. In a way, it's really quite fun."

She laughed. "If you say so."

"I do," he told her.

Abigail opened the house door and he followed her in, and past the stack of blankets folded on a chair. Last night, he'd slept here, in the kitchen area. He'd made himself a comfortable spot with the spare blankets, though he hadn't really slept much.

It wasn't because he was on the floor, it was honestly a mixture of things. Worry over Abigail's injuries, and fear she might actually leave and become a mail-order bride. Then, there was his anxiousness that someone might come in the middle of the night to try and hurt her or the children. He'd barely dozed, and got up several times to check the windows.

Being awake had also given him time to reflect on things. A small measure of humility had been given to him. He'd arrived, planning to be an exceptional teacher. He still was—there was no doubt in his mind about that. But he'd been surprised that the students, and their mother, had taught him.

It wasn't just enough to intend to change the trajectory of another's life. You had to be open to letting your own be changed as well.

Gaining friends, being accepted with open arms into another's family, and learning to get along with others and share your true self...it was just as important of a lesson as grammar or mathematics. Perhaps even more.

Though he'd never tell anyone else that.

Of course, there was also the other thing he'd reflected on. The fact he'd told Abigail just how he felt, and he hadn't heard a word from her yet. Each time, they'd been interrupted. It was frustrating, and he worried that perhaps that meant she wasn't the least bit interested in him.

They were keeping close to the house today, Abigail firm in her opinion the children needed to be indoors. Samuel had read to them, they'd all made lunch and a cornmeal cake together, and now the children were playing with the new kitten. There had been a little argument over the name that morning. Sally had wanted to call it Fluff Fluff. Little Jim had wanted Blackie. Thomas had said those names were babyish, and wanted to call it something more important, he just didn't know what.

Luckily, though not for him, when Abigail suggested they let him name it, the children had agreed. The first name to pop into Samuel's mind had been Panther, after the large black cat. It had, fortunately, delighted the children. Right now, they were teasing a piece of yarn along the ground, taking turns wiggling it while the kitten pounced on it.

Abigail checked on the cake in the oven, and everyone startled as there was a loud knock on the door. Samuel strode toward it, ready to protect Abigail and the children, when a voice called out, "It's the sheriff."

When he opened the door, Samuel was surprised to see it wasn't just the sheriff, but also Mr. Links.

"Gentlemen," he said with a nod.

"Hello, Mr. Donner. Might we have a word with you and Mrs. Lees?" the sheriff asked.

Abigail stepped forward and joined him in the front. He looked curiously at the small wagon pulled up in front of her house. Was Mr. Links making a delivery somewhere? It wasn't a far walk at all from the general store to here.

"Have you any news of the second man?" Abigail asked as she crossed her arms over her chest.

"Actually, yes," the sheriff said.

Abigail breathed out, "Thank goodness!"

"Who was he?" Samuel asked. "Do we need to worry further?"

"He's a hired gun," the sheriff answered. "And no, you don't. He's locked up and getting transported by a marshal tomorrow. Same with Mr. Sampson. Won't neither of them bother you again, ma'am. The other man told me and my deputy everything, and blamed Mr. Sampson for the theft and your assault and attempted kidnapping. Thomas will be cleared of all charges."

"I'm glad to hear it," Abigail said. Then, she turned to Mr. Links. "I hope you got your medal back."

"I did," he said, taking his hat off and holding it in his hands. "I came to apologize. And I'll tell everyone in town that we all need to apologize. I was wrong to accuse Thomas. I feel like a fool that I had any part in this. Mr. Sampson had been going around talking poorly about you, people were gossiping, and I...I'm ashamed that I let myself get pulled into all that."

He lowered his head. "I should have known better. The whole town should have. Gossip doesn't do anything but hurt the innocent. I'm hoping that you'll forgive me."

Abigail nodded. "I will. But I hope the next time I need to buy goods, it will be at your usual price."

"It will be," he told her. "And I brought some as an apology. Something else too, for your children."

"For the children?" Abigail shook her head slightly in confusion.

"Yes. Can they come out?" Mr. Links asked.

"I'll get them," Samuel said. He turned to the house, and a moment later, Thomas, Sally, and Little Jim stood near their mother.

"I've got something for you," Mr. Links said, putting his hat on his head and striding toward his wagon. "Thomas, for you, first, an apology. I should have known better. You've always been a good boy, and a helpful one when you ran errands for me. If you'll forgive me, I'd like to offer you an afterschool job. Regardless if you take it or not, I'd also like to give you this."

Samuel moved closer to Abigail and watched just as curiously as everyone else did. Mr. Links pulled out a fishing rod and a small box.

"Everything you need is right here," he said. "My gift as an apology to you."

"Oh no," Abigail gasped and shook her head. "That's too much. It's not necessary."

"I know it's not, but I won't feel right unless I try and make it up to you all." Mr. Links reached into his wagon again. "Sally, I have something for you."

The little girl drew closer, then let out a sob as Mr. Links deposited a beautiful doll into her arms. Sally cradled it, tears running down her cheeks. "Can I keep it, Ma?" she asked.

"My goodness," Abigail said, tears on her own face.

Samuel wrapped an arm around her shoulder, and Little Jim left her skirts to move closer. "Is there something for me?" he asked.

"Jim," his mother scolded.

But Mr. Links talked over her. "Sure is. Got one hundred new marbles in this sack," he told the boy. "Some real nice ones."

"Oh wow!" Little Jim shouted. He threw himself at the shopkeeper, wrapping his little arms around the man's waist. "Thank you, Mr. Links. Boy, you can blame Thomas any time you like, if we get surprises like this!"

Everyone laughed, even Thomas. Mr. Links reached into his wagon once more.

"Mrs. Lees," he told her. "I brought you something too."

"No," Abigail said. "That's where I draw the line."

"Now don't say that," he told her. "I'm doing what a good neighbor should have done sooner. Mr. Donner, give me a hand?"

Unsure of what the store owner wanted, Samuel walked over to the wagon. Inside were several large sacks of flour.

Abigail appeared next to him, and wiped her eyes. "You are too generous," she said.

"No, I'm a fool who should have known better," Mr. Links said. "You mark my words, I'll be telling everyone I was wrong. You're a good woman, Mrs. Lees. A fine mother. I'm right sorry for my mistake."

"There's nothing to forgive," Abigail said.

Samuel hauled the sacks of flour into the house and smiled as Little Jim examined his marbles, Sally rocked her doll, and Thomas dug through the box of fishing supplies. When the last sack was carried in, Mr. Links and the sheriff waved goodbye and headed back to town.

"My goodness," Abigail said as she stared at her children. "I'm a little in disbelief right now."

"It's a good ending to this tale," Samuel said. "Mr. Sampson and his accomplice are in jail and being taken away. Thomas's name was cleared, the children have been surprised with wonderful gifts, and you've got your flour. Flour for months, likely."

She laughed, and he admired how her eyes crinkled slightly at the corners, and her face transformed. Over the last few weeks, he'd seen too much sadness on Abigail's face. This was much better.

"There's one more thing, though," Abigail said. She looked up at him. "I owe you an answer," she said.

Samuel felt his stomach clench. His heart started to pound, and his chest felt tight. What was Abigail going to tell him?

Chapter 20

The look on Samuel's face might have made Abigail laugh, had this not been such a serious moment. His lips were pursed, as though he'd been given a spoonful of salt instead of sugar, his face was ashen, and his hands went to his stomach.

She couldn't help but, again, think what a contrast he was to her first impression. Before, he'd been so stiff, so awkward...now, he laughed, smiled, seemed relaxed, as though he fit right in and always had.

In truth, there were many times that Abigail had forgotten he wasn't a permanent fixture here in Cottonwood Falls, or in her life. How was it he hadn't always been here? He'd slipped right in—well, barged—but somehow, it had all worked out so well. The children liked him, she liked him...

No. That wasn't right at all. She more than liked him. Still, even though he'd told her how he felt, she had doubts. Worries. Was that natural? After all, she'd not gotten to choose her first relationship. Abigail really didn't know what to expect or how to act with a second one.

Other than truthful. Because that was all she could be. Abigail took a deep breath as she stepped outside and he followed her. "About what you said earlier. When we were alone."

"Yes?" His eyes were fixed on her, so focused, so intent, Abigail almost looked away.

"I've...never really had a relationship before with anyone of my own choosing. Romantic, I mean. I'm not wanting to confuse gratitude with friendship or with something more." She looked at him pleadingly. "But at the same time, when you are here, everything feels right. It's very confusing for me, and I think that might not be fair to you."

Samuel's pinched expression eased slightly. "I admit, I've also never had a relationship with someone. Not romantic, I mean. Not even a deep and true friendship like I feel with you. At least," he swallowed hard, "I hope that we are friends."

"I hope so too," Abigail said, lowering her head. "I'd like to be."

"I feel confused too," Samuel admitted. "This all feels normal. Natural. Like I want to do it every day of my life." He swept his gaze around her property. "Seeing this every day, seeing you every day, a man could grow used to it. To seeing your smile and happiness, to hearing the children laugh. Evenings together reading or talking. The idea just...it seems right. I don't know how to say it any way other than that. I hope that doesn't sound foolish." He looked at her with a perplexed expression. "For a teacher, you'd think perhaps I would be better with my words."

Abigail laughed. She reached for his hand and held it for a moment. There was so much she wanted to say, but she also wasn't sure how to.

They stood there quietly, and a gentle breeze washed over them. For some odd reason, it felt like the wind was carrying away all of the old. Bringing with it a second chance.

"Yes," Abigail said, looking up at him.

"Yes, what?"

"That's my answer. When you first told me how you felt, I needed time to think. To sort out my thoughts and feelings. But I did, and realized how empty my life would be without you in it." Abigail studied him for a moment. "I only hope that my answer hasn't come too late."

Samuel's face changed in an instant, to one of relief, then joy. He pulled her close, and Abigail reveled in his strong arms around her. "I'm at a loss for words," he said. "Other than I'm so happy right now."

Abigail leaned back slightly, and found her smile met with one of his.

"I will never leave your side," Samuel told her. "I will love you with all of my heart. And," he grimaced, "I will also one day have to thank your aunt, won't I? Since it was she who brought me here."

Abigail giggled. "If you don't, she'll be sure to loudly tell everyone how ungrateful you are, as she got you both a job and a wife."

He sighed. "I know you are right. Very well then. Tomorrow, I will thank her. But this evening is ours. I want to spend each moment of it with you. The same as I will do forever."

"I can't think of anything better," Abigail answered him.

"I can," Samuel said, arching an eyebrow. "It's something I've been wanting to do." At her small head shake of questioning, he leaned down and gently brushed his lips against hers. "I love you, Abigail."

"I love you, Samuel."

Epilogue

It had been a long day. Abigail was exhausted. That morning, she and Samuel had gotten married before what felt like half of the town. Her aunt had loudly carried on, making sure to tell everyone how she just knew Samuel was the perfect husband for Abigail. That's why she'd sent away for him.

Willy had been at her side, nodding along, and occasionally putting an arm around her aunt. Abigail sensed a new relationship on the horizon.

After their ceremony, the town gathered for a large feast. Her aunt had arranged it, and a cake too, so Abigail hadn't had to worry about a thing. Each townsperson had brought something, and everyone gathered, ate, laughed, talked, and danced until near sunset.

As Abigail, Samuel, and the three children walked back to their house, Abigail was sure she'd never felt so happy in her life. Samuel's hand had captured hers, and their steps matched.

Little Jim was yawning, while Sally hummed and danced with herself. Only Thomas was quiet. Glum, almost sullen.

"Thomas, what's the matter?" Abigail asked once they'd returned to the house.

Samuel and the other two children had gone inside, and she wrapped an arm around him. "I thought you liked Samuel. Are you upset that we are married now?"

"Oh, I like him well enough, like him a lot. But, Ma, how would you like it if your teacher was your pa? That means there's no excuse not to do my homework."

Abigail laughed, swatted at him, and opened the door to the house. "There are very few reasons not to do your homework."

"Yes, Ma," he grumbled as he walked inside.

Samuel came out of the house then, and glanced at the sky. "It's going to be a beautiful sunset," he said.

"Do you like to watch them?" Abigail asked as they settled on a bench and she rested her head on his shoulder.

"I do."

"I've never had anyone to enjoy one with before," Abigail said as the sun lowered and vibrant oranges and reds filled the horizon.

"Never?" he asked. At her head shake he said, "You do now." Then he asked, "Do you like watching rainstorms?"

"I do."

"I've never had anyone to enjoy one with before," Samuel said as he looked at her.

"You do now." Abigail rested her head back on his shoulder, and they sat in a perfect silence as the sun set, stars rose, and their new life together began.

If you enjoyed this story, you might want to spend more time in Cottonwood Falls and Spring Creek Falls

Caroline

Caroline Watson has been living at Mrs. Hardy's School for Girls since she was orphaned. When forced into marriage by the headmistress, she plots a desperate escape the night before to the furthest place her money will take her.

Even as he tells himself he is uninterested in the beautiful brunette who appeared off the stagecoach like an angel, Dr. Edward Mason finds himself attracted to Caroline. Still, he's determined that no one is going to tempt him into a relationship ever again.

Pushed together, Edward offers Caroline a job. Just as she's comfortable and settled in, a strange man comes to town and follows her. Now she's faced with a choice. Ask for help or run again.

https://www.amazon.com/Caroline-Runaway-Brides-West-Book/dp/B0BF3884CD

Asher's Secret

The plan? Pretend he's her betrothed and try not to fall in love.

Sheriff Asher Steele doesn't plan to settle down. Not ever. In fact, he avoids the ladies all together. And he doesn't plan to explain why that is. No one's been able to break through the walls of his emotions and that's just the way he likes it.

But when Isabelle Bowman comes to town with a secret of her own, and a heap of trouble following her, he might be the only one who can help her. What he's not counting on is falling in love along the way and considering opening the walls of his heart to protect her.

Running from her half-brother, who desires nothing more than to kill Isabelle Bowman and take her inheritance, she's desperate for a place to hide. Uninterested in marriage, she thinks the sheriff's idea is preposterous. But she's left with no option. With no funds, a sheriff who thinks she's a troublemaker or a liar, and his plan that will never work, she's sure things are not going to end well.

But could they both be wrong about what the future holds?

https://www.amazon.com/Ashers-Secret-Winning-Devotion-Book-ebook/dp/B0CK5GW81M

Note from Author

Thank you for taking the time to read Mail-Order Teacher!

Could I ask for one small favor? Reviews like yours on Amazon mean so much to me and help others to find my books! Even just a single line means a lot!

Also...

Want a FREE book?

Stop by my website to get your no strings attached **FREE book**. It's my gift to you, as a thank you for reading this one.

www.sarahlambbooks.com

About the Author

Sarah is wife to an amazing teacher and mom to two boys who are growing up just a little too fast. She spends her days working and writing in the Blue Ridge Mountains.

There are other great books in this series as well!

Find all the Mail-Order Husbands on Amazon!

https://www.amazon.com/dp/B0CKV92Y7D

***

Also by Sarah Lamb in this series

***

Mail-Order Gambler

Kody Hall lives life on a roll of the dice, betting on everything except love. He's learned the hard way that women don't mix well with gambling men. But he's willing to wager everything he has on a chance to change lives at the orphanage he secretly founded. He's also hoping the woman he's been corresponding with might be interested in taking a chance on a mail-order husband. He'd like to settle down.

Susan Louden, the orphanage's teacher, is fiercely protective of her charges. When she spots Kody, the town's notorious gambler, lurking around the grounds, she chases him off. In her eyes, gambling and innocence don't mix. Why can't more men be like the one she's been writing to?

But a surprise revelation about Kody's true intentions, and his identity, throws Susan's world into disarray. Could she have been wrong about him? The more she learns, the more she questions her own place in the orphanage, especially as she starts to develop feelings for him. Can a woman dedicate her life to children while being associated with a gambler?

It's something Kody's willing to gamble on.

https://www.amazon.com/gp/product/B0D7FWML
DP

***

Mail-Order Tailor

Josiah Adams, a single father burdened by a past betrayal, seeks refuge in the quiet town of Deepwater, answering the letter for a mail-order husband. He yearns for a mother for his young daughter, Madeline, but the ghosts of his failed marriage keep him guarded. He thinks he'll try again, but when he arrives, the woman who sent the letter is nowhere to be found.

Ginny Waters, the eldest of eleven, possesses a natural nurturing spirit. Drawn to Madeline's innocent charm, she takes on the role of nanny until the mysterious letter sender can be found. Meanwhile, her heart warms to both the little girl and her reserved father.

Their lives intertwine in a comfortable routine, and Josiah finds himself softening toward Ginny. Could there be room for love in his heart again? But what about the woman he was supposed to have a marriage of convenience with?

Suddenly, Madeline and Ginny vanish without a trace, the sender of the mail-order husband letter is made known, and Josiah's world crumbles. Fear and desperation grip him as he searches for answers. Will he ever see his daughter and his new love again?

https://www.amazon.com/stores/Sarah-Lamb/author/B098H3SGLK

Want more of Sarah's books?

Find them all on Amazon!
https://www.amazon.com/stores/Sarah-Lamb/auth
or/B098H3SGLK